# HELLRAISER

## YOU CAN ONLY GET THIS FEELING FROM A THUG

# K.L. HALL

Visit bit.ly/readBLP to join our mailing list for sneak peeks and release day links!

Let's connect on social media!

Facebook - B. Love Publications

Twitter - @blovepub

Instagram - @blovepublications

**We hate errors, but we are human! If the B. Love team leaves any grammatical errors behind, do us a kindness and send them to us directly in an email to blovepublications@gmail.com with ERRORS as the subject line.**

**As always, if you enjoyed this book, please leave a review on Amazon/Goodreads, recommend it on social media and/or to a friend, and mark it as READ on your Goodreads profile.**

# CONTENTS

# SYNOPSIS

When I set my sights on investigating an outlaw motorcycle gang, I wanted to write a groundbreaking story that would course-correct my journalism career.

I didn't expect the three things that followed:

1: Being stranded on the side of the road with a steaming car and dead cell.

2: Being preyed upon by a gang of leather-clad outlaws in a bar.

3: Being rescued by a dangerously handsome biker who's determined to do whatever to keep me safe.

Dreyson "Hellraiser" Moore is the gray-eyed vice president of the Hell's Savages.

The first time in his presence, I can tell he's got a thing for playing hero, even if he doesn't.

He says he's everything I should steer clear of, but since I'm being kept under his protection *and* sleeping in his bed, he's hard to avoid.

Soon, we find ourselves entwined in a whirlwind love story that takes our hearts by storm.

Immersed in his world, he's changing me in ways I never anticipated, leading me down a path I never planned.

He's all I crave, and I'm powerless to stop it.

"*Shit*," I hissed as my car started to sputter before coming to a steaming halt.

I stood outside my hot car on the side of a deserted back road, feeling the cool evening air bite at my butterscotch brown skin through my blouse. I couldn't fucking believe my luck. My car had broken down in the middle of a deserted stretch of road on the way home from meeting with a whistleblower with crucial information about a major sex trafficking scandal being done by a local MC, the Chicago Outlaws. To protect the witness's identity, I agreed to meet them in a secluded location two hours away, which eventually led to the thick-colored smoke emitting from my vehicle.

I drove an older diamond-white Toyota Camry that I'd lovingly named Pearl. She was practical but aging to the point where she'd become unreliable. She'd seen better days, with a few dents and scratches around the bumper and doors from years of wear and tear.

"You've really done it this time, old girl," I muttered while leaning over the hood as if I knew exactly what to look for.

Frustration and anxiety bubbled up inside me as I quickly realized I had no idea how to fix the problem. Not to mention, my phone was dead, I had no charger, and my GPS was utterly useless without four reliable wheels.

*Great. Just fucking great. Of all the times for this to happen...*

I'd been working my ass off to redeem myself after a significant career setback six months ago, after I ran with a story with a quote from a source that turned out to be false, which resulted in a big-ass defamation lawsuit for my company and cost me my job. The article I was writing for my new employer could make or break my journalism career. And if I didn't turn it into my editor by midnight, I was going to be even more royally fucked than I already was.

"Why me, God?" I quizzed, looking up at the sky.

I knew he had to be up there in Heaven having a hearty laugh at my expense.

After deciding I had no other option but to use the two feet he'd blessed me with, I grabbed my small crossbody bag with my essentials and started walking. I was thankful I'd paired my simple white blouse and forest green dress pants with sturdy boots instead of heels and that my hair was away from my face—pulled back into a sleek ponytail that stopped in the middle of my back.

The long road stretched before me, dark and empty, with no sign of life. I walked for what felt like hours, the cool air seeping into my bones with each step. Feeling drained and cold, I spotted the flickering neon lights of a bar in the distance.

*Thank you, Lord.*

Relieved, I headed toward it, hoping to find help. I pushed open the door, too tired to notice that I'd forgotten to remove my press badge after the interview. The warm air and noise hit me like a tidal wave. The place was crawling with rough-looking men. Not just any men—bikers. Their eyes followed me as I walked in. I felt a chill race down my spine but tried to appear confident. I kept my head held high, determined not to show how fucking nervous I was, as I proceeded over to the bartender.

The interior was far from any place I'd ever stepped foot in. It was dimly lit, with a few flickering neon signs scattered across the room. The air was thick with the smell of stale liquor, smoke, and something else I couldn't quite place—something musty and sour like a mixture of vomit and tequila. My shoes stuck to the floor, and I had to resist the urge to look at what was causing it.

The bar counter was dark and scarred from years of drunk ass patrons. Behind it were shelves lined with various liquor bottles. An old jukebox played an old country tune in the back corner, the music barely audible.

"Excuse me, c-can I use your p-phone?" I stuttered as I approached the counter. "My car broke down way down the road, and I need to make a call."

The bartender was a burly man with long, fuzzy locs, a grizzly beard, and what looked like a permanent grimace. His lip curled in a twisted smirk that creeped me out.

"Sorry, lil lady. Ain't no phone here," he answered, eyes lingering on me too long for my liking.

His response was curt but still made my skin prickle. Still, I didn't know if I was more disappointed or relieved to have not received any help. I glanced over my shoulder. All eyes were still stationed on me. The patrons were all rugged, and the room was full of brooding bikers who seemed to have made this place their home away from home. They sat scattered around cocktail tables and booths across the room. By the looks on their faces, it was a place where strangers weren't welcomed, and my uninvited presence had noticeably disrupted the vibe.

I felt the weight of their stares, and my anxiety heightened. It wasn't a place a young woman like me should've been in alone, especially not one on a desperate mission. *I gotta get the fuck out of here.*

"Thanks," I said quickly.

I turned to leave, only to lock eyes with a young female who didn't look to be a day older than fifteen. She was carrying a tray full of drinks, had on a skimpy waitressing uniform, and way too much damn makeup. It screamed, *I'm trying to look older than I really am.*

From the neck down, she looked like a good time, but one look into her eyes, and all I saw staring back at me was a scared child. Before I could say anything to her, I found my path blocked by a biker with a patch on his leather jacket that said President and a menacing grin. The one percent patch on his jacket was apparent, signaling that he was part of a gang that separated themselves from other law-abiding riders, and it became clear my safety was far from guaranteed. He was the president of the Chicago Outlaws, the MC at the epicenter of my article. My heart stumbled out a frantic beat as the heavily tattooed man wrapped his waist around the young girl, whispered something in her ear, and smacked her ass before she disappeared into the back. By the time I blinked, he'd grabbed my arm. His grip was unyielding.

"You lost, lil lady?" he asked, noticing my press badge. Before I could answer, he reached out to snatch it from my waist. He glanced at it, and his eyes narrowed to slits. "Mercy Harris, huh? What's a pretty lil thing like you doing in a place like this?"

Terror had me in its clutches as the other bikers started to close in. Their vulgar comments made my skin crawl. I glanced away, trying to think of an excuse quickly.

"I'm just passing through," I explained, trying to keep my voice steady. "Having a little car trouble, that's all."

The man leaned in closer with the group of men at his six.

"Passing through, huh? Ain't nothing for you to find here but trouble. Or maybe that's why you're here, to start nosing around in shit that ain't none of your fuckin' business."

I stuttered, trying to explain myself, when the menacing figure snatched my bag from my shoulder. I watched helplessly as he dumped its contents onto a nearby table, scattering my notebooks, pens, sticky notes, and voice recorder. He laughed and made crude comments as he rummaged through my things.

He swiped up my voice recorder, studying it with a scornful grin. "Sorry, Oprah. No stories here," he taunted menacingly.

"No, please wait," I called out to him.

But I was too late. He threw it to the ground and stomped on it, smashing it to pieces under his thick black boot. My heart clunked to my feet, having to witness my crucial evidence being destroyed as the pieces of my recorder scattered across the floor.

All my hard work—doing the research, preparing the questions, risking it all to meet my source to have my inquiries answered— seemed to have slipped through my fingers like grains of sand. Knowing I hadn't had the chance to transcribe or upload the recording to the cloud made the loss even more devastating. All that I'd worked so hard to obtain was gone.

"Consider this a warning," the biker growled, leaning in close. "You know what we do to snitches around here, especially when they're as pretty as you?" he asked menacingly.

Fear clawed at my throat as dread consumed me. I knew I should've thought of ways to bounce back from the setback. After all, pivot was my middle name. I couldn't afford to give up because giving up meant getting fired… *again*. The thought of losing my job and the career I'd worked so hard to rebuild was almost overwhelming enough to make me scream.

I had to find another way to get the information I needed for the story. It was the only way I'd be able to prove to myself that I had the chops to make it in journalism, and see the Outlaws fall for the things they'd done to women. *If* I survived the night in the presence of those monsters, I'd take it as a sign to turn my lemons into lemonade. But that was a big ass if. I closed my eyes and prayed to God almighty for a miracle, hoping for a way out of my fucked-up situation.

*At least if I die, I'll still have a story that ends up on the newspaper's front page.*

I SAT ON MY BIKE, hidden in the shadows of an alley across the street from the Outlaws' Den—a notorious bar belonging to our rival MC, the Chicago Outlaws. As the vice president of the Hell's Savages, I'd taken it upon myself to handle the surveillance mission personally. My father, president of the Hell's Savages, expected nothing but perfection from me, and I was determined to prove my worth.

The cool air blew past me, getting colder as the sun went down. I remained focused, my eyes trained on the bar's entrance. I'd been here for hours, watching for any signs of unusual activity. The Outlaws had been getting bolder lately, going from drug trafficking to selling women, and I needed to find out what they were planning next.

As I considered calling it a night, I spotted a lone figure walking down the road. It was a woman with a swinging ponytail and her arms wrapped tightly around herself, shivering from the cold. She looked out of place, too innocent for the rough crowd that frequented the Outlaws' Den.

My heart sank half a foot as I watched her slow her stride as she gazed at the bar's entrance. She hesitated for a moment.

*What the hell are you doing out here, girl? Keep walking. You don't want any part of this. Don't go inside. Don't do it. Don't do it. Fuck. She did it.*

She pushed open the door and stepped inside. I groaned while rubbing my temple in frustration.

*Just what I fuckin' needed. Now I have to worry about you too.*

I watched the scene unfold from the shadows, feeling an intense internal pull to go in and save her. I knew it would blow my cover, jeopardizing the mission, but I couldn't stand by and let her get hurt or worse. I'd seen what the Outlaws did to women, and the thought of that innocent creature falling into their hands filled me with a cold rage. She wouldn't stand a mothafuckin chance.

I knew I couldn't let her wander straight into the lion's den without protection. I quickly texted Prez—my father—asking for backup. I needed my brothers to ensure shit didn't turn into a full-scale war. After sending the message, I tucked my phone away and focused on the task.

I hopped off my bike with my Glock in tow and headed across the street, sticking to the shadows until I reached the bar's entrance. I gulped down a steadying breath, mentally preparing myself for the chaos I was sure would unfold as soon as I burst through the door. The bar was as seedy as I expected, filled with a crowd of rough-looking niggas and a thick cloud of marijuana smoke. I spotted the woman standing a few feet from the bar, her expression riddled with fear.

My gray eyes narrowed as I saw Cannon, their president, grab her arm. He started mumbling something to her, but I didn't need to hear his words. The terror in her eyes told me all I needed to know.

I stepped forward without wasting any more time, instantly drawing attention and sticking out like a sore thumb. The room fell silent for a split second as everyone turned to look at me.

"Get your fuckin' hands off her. Now," I demanded, voice booming over the music and murmurs.

Cannon snapped his neck in my direction, and looked me up and down, his grip on the woman's brown wrist tightening.

"Seems to me you're in the wrong mothafuckin bar, nigga. You think you can just walk in here and start dishing out orders? Your authority don't matter here.

Without hesitation, I reached for the gun on my hip and fired a warning shot into the ceiling, my eyes dead-locked on Cannon's. The sudden noise startled the bikers, but it wasn't enough to make them back down, their intentions clear.

"I said, let her go. Or I'll make sure you fuckin' regret it."

Cannon hesitated, assessing the situation. The tension in the room was apparent, and I was outnumbered a million to one, but after a long moment, he released his grip on her. She stumbled back, grabbing her wrists to rub away the pain. The fear in her eyes was replaced by relief as she locked her gaze on me.

The woman was initially frozen in shock. Soon after, she ducked behind an overturned table, keeping her head down and trying to make herself as invisible as possible. Before I could grab her, the room quickly plummeted into chaos as the bikers charged at me. Punches were thrown left and right. All hell broke loose as some bikers grabbed bottles from the bar, smashing them to use as weapons during the brawl. All I heard was the sound of breaking glass around me.

In the heat of the brawl, tables were flipped over, sending drinks flying. The floor was a slippery mess with spilled liquor and broken glass, making it difficult to maintain my balance.

Still, I fought through the crowd, dodging flying fists and debris as I forced my way through the madness. My fists were bloodied as I used a combination of flying punches and kicks with my gun at the ready. One of the bikers grabbed a chair and swung it at me, connecting with my back. The heavy wooden chair splintered upon impact, adding to the debris scattered across the floor.

Just as things started to look grim, a few of my MC brothers burst through the door, coming to my defense with bullets and blows. Their brutal reinforcements gave me the edge I needed. I fought my way to the woman, roughly grabbing her hand and pulling her toward the exit as my brothers held off the remaining bikers.

"Come on. We need to get the fuck out of here!"

She followed me closely, trusting me to usher her to safety. She kept her head low and moved quickly, avoiding the chaos.

More of my brothers were coming, but we couldn't wait. I wouldn't let her become another victim. I pushed through the chaos, finally reaching the door and bursting into the cold night air. Once outside, she clung to me like a second skin as I led her to my motorcycle and quickly helped her onto the back before passing her my helmet for safety.

"Put it on and hold on tight," I instructed.

As the engine roared to life, I peeled out of the alley, tires squealing. The wind whipped past us as we sped away from the bar, the woman clinging tightly to me. I felt her petite body trembling, but I knew she was safe with me.

We rode off into the night, leaving the danger and chaos behind. My heart bucked against its reins, but I felt a sense of relief knowing I could protect her.

*I might've blown my cover, but I'd do it all over again to save her, and I don't even know her fucking name.*

As we sped away from the bar, I clung to the handsome stranger, my heart throbbing recklessly with fear. The cold night air whipped my hair past my face, but I barely felt it. My mind was still reeling from the chaos we'd escaped and being saved by my unlikely hero. As the bar faded into the background, I slowly processed what happened.

*Who is this man, and why did he save me?*

As we rode, I saw the patch on his leather jacket. It was different from the ones the other bikers wore inside the bar. The emblem stood out—a demonic dog with fiery red eyes and sharp teeth set to strike. Below it, the words "Hell's Savages MC" were embroidered in bold, red letters.

*Hell's Savages… I've heard of them. They were rivals to the Chicago Outlaws. But why would he risk his life to save me?*

My mind raced, connecting the dots of what I'd witnessed. The story I'd been chasing—the rumors of the Chicago Outlaws trafficking women—had always seemed like whispers in the dark. But after what I witnessed in that bar, the insight hit me like a punch in the gut. It was all true. Every man in there all but undressed me with their stomach churning glares. *The Chicago Outlaws are trafficking women. I saw that young girl with my own eyes. This is the story I've been looking for that could bring my career back from the dead.*

I'd been following a lead, hoping to uncover the truth. Never in a million years did I expect to be thrust straight into the middle of it. The fear I felt inside that bar was mixed with a burning determination to expose the Outlaws for the sick criminals they were and finally seal an internal wound that had never healed. Somehow, I hoped by bringing justice to the women they'd harmed, that would somehow suffice for me as well since the teacher who'd sexually violated me in high school never saw repercussions for his heinous actions.

As we rode through the night, I tightened my grip around the vigilante's waist, feeling a strange sense of safety despite the danger we'd narrowly escaped. Words couldn't express how grateful I was for his intervention. I owed him my life.

We rode for what felt like an eternity before he finally slowed down, pulling off the road and into a secluded spot. He cut the engine, and the sudden silence was almost deafening. I drowned my lungs with air, trying to steady my disorderly heart as I lifted the helmet off my head.

The man turned to me, his expression filled with concern. "Are you okay?"

I nodded, still trying to find my voice. "I-I think so. Thank you. Y-you saved my life. I don't know what I would've done without you."

His piercing gray eyes softened slightly, complementing his smooth, rich brown skin. Still, his demeanor remained serious. It was the first time I'd gotten a good look at him up close. A well-proportioned nose sat in the middle of his angular face with thick well-groomed brows that framed his captivating gray eyes. My gaze dropped to his full lips and thick beard that wrapped around his jawline, adding to his commanding presence.

His long locs were freshly twisted at the roots and styled in thick individual braids that stopped in the center of his muscular chest. He had a muscular build with broad shoulders and was tall enough to easily stand out in a crowd.

"You shouldn't have been there in the first fuckin' place. What were you thinking? That bar is dangerous, especially for someone like you."

Feeling embarrassed, I looked away as he scolded me.

"I know. My car broke down, and I was trying to find a phone to call for help. I didn't realize what kind of place it was."

He ran a hand through his long dreads, frustration evident in his chiseled expression.

"You need to be more careful. Those mothafuckas wouldn't have hesitated to hurt you, rape you, or worse."

I shivered at the thought, reverting to the terrifying moments inside the bar.

"I understand. But why did you help me? You're wearing a different patch. You're with the Hell's Savages, right?"

He nodded, his eyes locking onto mine. "Dreyson. Niggas call me Hellraiser, but you can call me Dre." He introduced himself. "I'm the VP."

"Mercy," I replied. "Mercy Harris."

"And yeah, I'm with the Hell's Savages, but we say the Savages. And I couldn't just stand by and let them hurt you. It didn't sit right with me."

A surge of gratitude and relief bloomed inside me. I saw why he'd gotten the name Hellraiser. Despite the danger, this man—Dre

—and his MC brothers had raised Cain and Abel, and risked everything to save me. I took a deep breath, deciding to trust him with the truth.

"Thank you again. I'm a journalist. I've been investigating rumors about the Outlaws trafficking women. The last thing I expected was to find myself in the middle of it."

His expression hardened, anger flashing in his gray eyes.

"You're lucky you got out of there alive. Those mothafuckas are ruthless. But if you're looking for proof, I guess you've got it now."

I nodded, feeling a renewed sense of purpose before remembering my proof was gone. "People need to know what's going on, which is even more reason for me to get this story out. But that maniac back there destroyed my recorder."

"What you need to do is be careful. The Outlaws won't take kindly to being exposed, but I think you already know that."

I turned to him, my voice trembling slightly as I tried to steady my nerves. "Um, you think you could take me back to my car? I can wait for AAA there."

He shook his head, his expression serious. "No. It's not safe."

My heart pitter-pattered against my ribcage. "What? Why not?"

He looked into my eyes. "The Outlaws will be looking for you and me. Too many bodies dropped tonight. They won't let what went down slide."

My eyes popped wide as saucers. Fear coursed through me as the gravity of the situation started to bake itself into my brain. *Fuck.* That nightmare of a man had taken my badge, which meant he had my full name and credentials and knew where I worked.

"Oh my God… That man took my press badge. He'll know who I am."

"And he won't hesitate to send his men after you."

His chilling warning set off every alarm inside my body. "What do you mean? But what am I supposed to do? M-my car is broken down. I don't have a charger. I don't have a—"

Dre drew in a deep breath, his mind made up. "I can help you, but you need to trust me. For now, you'll have to come home with me. It's the only way I'll be sure you're safe until we figure this shit out. Now, put your helmet back on."

I worriedly looked into his gray eyes and saw a blend of uncertainty and determination staring back at me. Despite the fear churning inside my gut, I felt safe with him. Dre revved the engine before I could object and took off again seconds later. The wind whipped past my face as we sped through the night. I held onto his waist for dear life as my mind raced with thoughts.

*How the hell did I end up in this situation, and what will happen to me now? What happened to that girl?*

As we rode, I tried to lull my anxiety by focusing on the warmth of Dre's rock-hard body, the steady hum of the motorcycle, and reminding myself that he'd saved me once. I had to believe he'd continue to keep his promise.

I PULLED UP TO THE SAVAGES' clubhouse. The familiar sight of the weathered brick building brought a sense of relief to me, causing me to exhale a breath I didn't even know I'd been holding. I killed the engine and helped Mercy off my bike, guiding her inside with my hand around her dainty wrist.

As always, the clubhouse was bustling with the regular activity —drinking, smoking, and shit-talking over games at the pool table now that the threat had been neutralized. At least for now. All eyes turned to me as we entered. My father stood overhead, waiting for me with a concerned expression.

"Come with me," I muttered to her.

I led Mercy to my spacious bedroom at the back of the clubhouse. I gestured for her to sit on the bed. It was a sturdy queen-size sleigh bed with a dark wooden frame. The bedding was simple, including a slate gray comforter and matching sheets. At least I kept it made. I set my Glock on top of the small nightstand next to it.

"Stay here. Don't leave this room."

Mercy jerked her head forward in a nod, her brown gaze wide with uncertainty. I had to admit she had a beautiful oval-shaped face and naturally glowing caramel skin with a yellow undertone. Long, thick eyelashes sat over her cocoa-brown, almond-shaped eyes. Her thick, perfectly arched eyebrows and button nose framed her face perfectly, and her full lips had an inviting heart shape.

I dipped my chin before closing the door behind me and heading to my father's office. The cold tension enveloped me as soon as I stepped inside. He was seated behind his large, dark mahogany desk in a worn, high-backed leather chair. There was a large, detailed map of the city in front of him, with strategic locations and territories we controlled.

The walls that enveloped us were lined with memorabilia of our club's legacy—framed photos of our members, black and white images of some of my father's favorite vintage motorcycles, and various plaques and awards.

"What the *fuck* were you thinking, Hellraiser?" he growled.

I took a deep breath, knowing I had to come correct.

"I was thinking about living up to my name, Prez. I couldn't deal with the guilt if she'd gotten hurt. We both know what the Outlaws do to women, especially ones as beautiful as her. She's a journalist, and she wants to write an article and expose them for sex trafficking women. This might be a blessing in disguise."

My father's brown eyes narrowed, a blend of frustration and understanding. "She's your responsibility now. All you did was make her fate worse, especially if she writes that fucking article."

I grunted while looking around at the heavy wooden bookshelves lined against the opposite side of the room. He wasn't wrong. I knew the risks of exposing the Outlaws but also understood the importance of bringing their heinous crimes to light. I hated those bitch-made mothafuckas with everything in me and wanted nothing more but to see them fall, but there was no telling what kind of hell Mercy's article would unleash.

A wave of anger rolled through me, causing me to storm out of the office. I stomped back to my room and pushed open the door. It thudded against the wall with a loud bang, startling Mercy. She'd transferred from the bed to my desk, scribbling furiously in one of my notebooks. She jumped before looking over her shoulder as I entered. Her eyes danced with determination.

"I've been writing down *everything* I saw at the Outlaws' Den," she urged. "Would you be comfortable going on record or at least letting me interview you about what you've seen regarding how the Outlaws treat women and the trafficking?"

I took a deep breath, quickly affirming my decision. "Look, I get it. You need a story, and you want to expose the Outlaws. But I can't help you that way. I'm not a snitch."

Disappointment flashed in her brown orbs.

"But I need evidence. Your statement could be crucial to—"

I swung my head, my expression firm as I cut her sentence off at the knees. "I said no. It's too fuckin' risky, and I've already risked a hell of a lot behind your ass, all right?"

Her perfectly arched brows furrowed as she sighed.

"But this story needs to be told," she protested. "I don't see why you're fighting me on this. I promise to keep your identity anonymous if you're worried about that."

"You think I'm worried about some lil fuckin' article? This shit... this world is much bigger and darker than your pretty lil ass even realizes. It's cute. But being cute won't cut it here," I growled, giving her the cold, hard truth.

Mercy smacked her full lips before she scoffed. "Whatever. I'll finish it with or without you."

"Listen up," I barked, switching subjects. "Here's how this shit is gonna go while you're here. You're my guest and under my sole protection. You'll sleep in my room and not mess with or even interact with *any* other guys in the club. You understand?"

Mercy looked at me with a blank stare. "Whoa. Wait. I thought this was just for the night, and you'd take me back to my car in the morning."

"We're past the point of that now, gorgeous. Keep up."

Her glare hardened as her expression clouded with fear and uncertainty. "What about my job? I'm on a deadline."

I sighed, running a hand through my locs. My eyes darted over to her phone charging on my nightstand.

"Make up a lie or call in sick. Do whatever you have to do to buy your ass some time. I don't know how long this will take to get the Outlaws off our backs. If I know them like I think I do, they'll want to make a deal soon enough."

Mercy nodded, slowly starting to understand the gravity of the situation. We'd put each other in difficult positions, and I *hated* how much she frustrated me, trying to fight me at every turn when I'd already said what I said. That shit made my dick brick up in my jeans. I really wanted to fuck all that back-talk and defiance right out of her. I hated that I couldn't stop imagining smashing her fuckin' pelvis and putting her ass through the fuckin' mattress. I hated how much arguing with her made me fuckin' want her. I hated how badly I wanted to hear the sound of her moan my name while I punished her fuckin' pussy.

I was at a crossroads. On the one hand, the beast in me wanted to bend her over, tear off her clothes, and bury all ten inches of my thick dick inside her. On the other hand, I knew I needed to stay far away from her. Aside from the occasional MC groupie or two, I didn't normally keep a woman around me like this, but there was something different about her. I couldn't help but want to shield her from all harm and had no clue why.

*I'll never let Cannon or any other nigga lay a hand on her.*

I left the room with haste, afraid of what I might've done if I remained in her presence. My legs didn't stop until they'd propelled me outside. The night air was cool as I marched to my truck, lighting a blunt. The dark sky was dotted with a few stars, and the sound of crickets chirping competed with the loud thoughts racing through my head.

I leaned against the back and took a deep drag, watching the orange ember glow in the dark. I heard the familiar crunch of gravel and twisted my neck to see Ghost, our enforcer, walking toward me while lighting his own blunt. He stood next to me in silence, watching the smoke curling up into the sky, the scent of marijuana fusing with the night air.

Ghost broke his silence, his voice low. "Quite a fuckin' scene tonight, huh?"

I grunted. "Did you get a final report from Doc? What's the damage?"

"A few broken bones, a few bruises, but hey, nobody died."

"Yeah."

"What about you? How'd you make out?"

It was the first time I'd thought about myself all night. My world began orbiting around Mercy the moment I saw her walk into that fuckin' bar. I looked down at myself, noticing the bloodstains on my shirt and a few open cuts on my hands from all the flying glass.

I shrugged. "I'm good."

"And the lady?"

I tensed up at the mention of Mercy. "She's good too."

"I hope she's worth it." We traded silent glances before Ghost continued. "So, what's our next move? The Outlaws will be looking for her, but you already know that."

I exhaled a curl of smoke as I contemplated the situation. Mercy was a wildcard, and I was prepared to go all in.

"She said she had car trouble. Get with Blaze and have him ride out with a few prospects to find and haul her car back here so he can take a look at it. The sooner we get it fixed, the better."

"And then?" he probed before pulling a long drag of his blunt.

I sighed. "I don't know. Right now, my gut is telling me we need to watch and wait and let shit cool off. As long as she's here at the clubhouse, she's safe."

Ghost nodded, understanding the gravity of the situation but still visibly on edge. He'd never been afraid to go to war, but he needed to know the who, the why, and the worth.

"Yeah, but for how long? The Outlaws may have eaten shit tonight, but you know those mothafuckas are ruthless. He knows you have her, and because you do, he'll come for her, and when he does, we both know he won't show restraint just because it's you."

I looked at Ghost, my expression unyielding. "He's not going to lay a fuckin' hand on her, all right? We'll keep her safe as if she were one of our own. As far as Cannon goes, that mothafucka may be dumb, but he's not stupid. He knows better than to step foot on our territory. Put the word out to everyone to stay alert. Have the prospects take shifts standing watch," I ordered.

Ghost took another puff of his blunt, the orange glow highlighting the gritty look on his scarred, melanated face.

"Orders received, boss. We'll watch her back. But if it comes down to it, we'll end up doing a lot more than watching and waiting. We need a goddamn plan," he urged.

I dipped my chin, appreciating his loyalty and readiness to go to war.

"If we have to go to war, then we go to war. No matter what, we won't falter, and we won't fail. We're Savages, and we'll get through this like we always do."

We fell back into a meditative silence, the uncertainty of war suspended in the air, wondering when our enemies would choose to strike. The distant rumble of motorcycles was an ever present reminder of the dangers we faced, of the war I'd started all because of one beautiful fuckin' damsel.

I took a shower while my phone charged and changed into an oversized T-shirt and sweatpants Dre had left for me on the bed. I didn't know whether to like or hate him, and I hadn't been in his presence for twenty-four hours.

I stepped over to my phone and hesitantly dialed my boss's number. As I explained my absence, trying to sound as sick as possible, I was quickly met with frustration on the other end.

"You're calling out sick? Do I have to remind you that you're still in your probationary period? This isn't the time to be unreliable."

I drew in a deep breath. "I'm sorry, but I feel horrible. My body aches everywhere, and I have a fever. I think it might be the flu. Can I *please* get an extension on the deadline, Mr. Charles? All I'm asking for is a few more days."

There was a pregnant pause, then a heavy, reluctant sigh. "Fine.

You can have a one-week extension, but this is your last chance. If you miss this deadline, you're done here. Got it?"

I felt a knot tighten in the pit of my stomach. Lord knows I didn't want to lose another job. "Understood. Thank you, sir."

I ended the call and sat there, wishing my situation was as simple or ordinary as the flu. My uncanny situation weighed down on me, and I started to feel sick to my stomach. I lay down, curling into the fetal position on the bed, eyes scanning Dre's room.

A large, dark wooden dresser was against one wall with a vintage motorcycle poster strung up above it. On top of it were a few of his items—a worn brown leather wallet, a set of keys, a gold Cuban link chain, and a framed patch from his MC. A pair of leather boots sat by the bedroom door, and a leather vest hung on a white hook.

I closed my eyes with thoughts of Dre dancing through my head. Who was he? How long would I be trapped under his protection? And how long until I stopped wishing it was all one big, bad dream?

With thoughts of him came the realization of the danger I was in. The memory of the Outlaws snatching my press badge, ruining my recording, and knowing my identity haunted me like a bad dream. I'd never be able to fall asleep. I needed something to calm my nerves and take the edge off.

The door creaked open, and Dre walked in, the scent of marijuana clinging to him like a second skin. I slowly opened my eyes and looked up, my gaze meeting his.

"You good?" he asked.

I shook my head slightly before clearing my throat. "Can't sleep. My anxiety is on ten, and I need something to mellow me out."

I was too afraid to tell him the truth—that my self-doubt had my mind in a fucking chokehold.

He nodded, empathetic to my need for some relief after the night we'd had. Reaching into his pocket, he pulled out a blunt and offered it to me.

"You smoke?"

I hesitated for a second before reaching out to take it. The gesture was unexpected, but I appreciated it. He nodded toward the door, and I got up to follow him. We headed outside to his truck, where the cool night air provided fresh air I didn't know I needed.

As we reached his truck, he draped his leather jacket over my shoulders, and the warmth and masculine scent of the leather comforted me in a way I had never expected. I took a deep breath, feeling a little more relaxed.

"Thank you."

He lit the blunt, the flame flickering in the darkness as he passed it to me. I took a quick drag, the thick smoke filling my lungs and easing my nerves. We stood in silence for a moment, the only sounds being the distant sounds from the clubhouse and the chirp of crickets and yowling of stray cats.

"You feeling better now?" he inquired.

I nodded, feeling a bit calmer and soothed by his presence and the warmth of his jacket. The ambiguity of the situation still loomed large, but for the moment, I felt a tiny fraction of peace.

"Y'know, I haven't smoked since college," I confessed.

"Honestly, I'm surprised you're holding your own and not over there coughing your head off."

"I've got good lungs," I said, passing the blunt to him.

He took a drag from it, the look in his eyes playful. "I bet you would've been a trip to see high back then."

I chuckled, remembering one of my high stories from my junior year in college. "I was. There was this one time when I had this philosophy paper due. Of course, I was dragging ass and waited until the night before to start a ten-page assignment. I had zero time management skills back then. Anyway, my roommate and I decided to pull an all-nighter, and she suggested smoking a blunt to get us locked in and focused."

Dre arched a questioning brow with an amused expression. "Weed to stay focused, huh? Yeah. Sounds like a real smart plan."

"Yeah. Looking back, it definitely wasn't the smartest idea, but at the time, it seemed brilliant. We sat in our living room with the blunt in hand, typing away on our laptops. The room was filled with smoke so thick we could barely see our screens," I reminisced.

Dre chuckled, his locs slightly shaking as he swung his head.

"So, did the blunt help you write a ten-page paper?"

I grinned before taking the blunt back and inhaling deeply.

"Hell no. About halfway through the night, we'd eaten up every damn snack in the apartment, and my roommate started feeling nauseous from all the junk food. She fell asleep hugging the toilet, and I passed out three and a half pages in on the couch."

Dre belted out a soft laugh, clearly amused by my story.

"Sounds like y'all had a rough ass night. Did you manage to finish the paper in time?"

"Barely. I shot awake a little after sunrise and immediately started trying to decipher what the hell I'd been trying to say the night before. I was writing and rewriting paragraphs until eleven thirty. It was due by noon."

"Did you pass?"

"Surprisingly, I got an A on that paper, so I guess the weed did influence it. That or the fear of failing when I woke up the next morning."

Dre continued to laugh. "Yo, that's wassup. At least all your hard work paid off in the end."

I smiled. "Yeah, those were the days. It's nice to reminisce about the sunnier side of things, especially with everything going on."

"Yeah. Good ol' memory lane."

I sighed. "I know I've said it already, but thanks for helping me, Dre. I don't know what I would've done if you hadn't been there."

"You're safe here, Mercy. I promise you that. We protect our own, and right now, that means you too."

I studied him momentarily, taking in the strong, rugged exterior he'd presented to me. But I sensed something about him, a softness beneath his hard shell.

"You act so tough, but I can tell you have a soft heart under that hard exterior."

Dre raised a questioning brow, a gleam of curiosity in his eyes. "What makes you think that?"

He passed the blunt back to me, and I took another slow tug, letting the smoke linger in the air as I gathered my thoughts before answering.

"I can only go off energy, and yours is different. I'm a complete stranger. Look at the way you're looking out for me. You wouldn't do that if you didn't have something golden beating behind your ribcage."

Dre examined me, a hint of a smirk playing at the corners of his mouth. "You're pretty insightful, you know that?"

I shrugged. "I'm a journalist. It comes with the territory. Besides that, I just call shit like I see it. And what I see when I look at you is a man who's tough on the outside because you feel like you have to be, but on the inside, you possess a heart of gold."

He didn't object. Instead, he fell into a relaxed silence as I watched the smoke from the blunt curl into the darkness. I felt a sense of peace I hadn't expected to find in such a high-stakes situation.

After our conversation and smoking the blunt down until it burned our fingertips, Dre and I headed back inside the clubhouse. My limbs felt heavy as I slid the jacket off my shoulders and lazily returned it to him. The warmth of the space made me feel tired, but suddenly, I realized how hungry I was. My stomach growled audibly, which caused me to giggle.

"I'm pretty sure I have the munchies real bad," I confessed.

Dre grinned, understanding the feeling. "Come on. We've got some leftover chili and cornbread one of the prospects made. It's pretty good."

He led me into the kitchen, and I hopped onto the counter, watching Dre move around to fix me a bowl. He pulled a pot from the fridge and started heating the leftover chili on the stove.

I noticed a bag of unopened Doritos on the counter as I waited. Unable to resist, I snatched it, tore it open, and munched away. The comforting, salty snack relieved my urgent hunger pains. After hearing the loud crunch of the chips between my teeth, Dre looked over his shoulder and caught me in mid-bite.

"Your hungry ass couldn't wait, huh?" he teased.

I grinned, unable to respond with a mouthful of Cool Ranch chips.

I swung my head in a no before covering my mouth before I spoke. "Nope. Too hungry."

Dre laughed, shaking his head as he stirred the chili.

"I guess I can't blame you. Those Cool Ranch chips do hit when you high."

I nodded in agreement. "Oh my God, right!"

"This chili's gonna taste even better now. Watch."

Soon, the scent of the well-seasoned chili wafted past my nose, causing my stomach to growl even louder. I continued snacking on the chips, enjoying the moment of lightheartedness between us.

After a few minutes, Dre scooped the steaming chili into a bowl and handed it to me with warmed square of cornbread and a spoon on the side.

"Here you go. Be careful, though. It's hot."

Eager to taste it, I took a spoonful, blowing on it to cool it down before putting it in my mouth. My tastebuds rejoiced at the flavors, and I nodded eagerly.

"Wow! This is *really* good."

"Worth the wait, right?"

"Oh, for sure."

Dre smiled, pleased to see me enjoying the food. "Glad you like it. A few of the Savages are talented cooks."

"Kudos to whoever made this, for real. It's amazing."

I savored the chili, feeling a bit more human with each spoonful. Sharing a blunt and a meal with Dre made me feel thankful for the small slice of normalcy amid the madness.

———

I woke up the following day to the bright sunlight filtering through the open gray curtains. The room was quiet, and for a second, I'd forgotten where I was and how much shit I was in. As I shifted and stretched under the sheets, I rolled over to see Dre sitting on the edge of the bed, shirtless and staring at me. The unexpected sight of him made me squeeze my thighs together. It was the first time he'd gotten that close since he brought me there, having avoided the bed altogether and barely spending any time in the room with me as if I had a contractible disease.

He grunted. "Good afternoon."

I yawned, rubbing the sleep from my eyes before reaching for my phone. "Afternoon? What time is it?"

"Almost two-thirty. You were tired, so I let you sleep."

The first thing I did was check my email. There was one from my boss. My heart somersaulted when I read the subject line, *URGENT: New Deadline*. I opened the email, quickly scanning its contents. My frustration grew with each word. Mr. Charles worded his email to make sure I felt the pressure.

"Fuck," I mumbled under my breath.

"You good? You look upset."

My eyes met his concerned gaze, and I shrugged while forcing a smile. "Just work stuff. My boss wasn't happy about me calling out last night. And if I don't meet my new deadline for this article, I'll be out of another job indefinitely."

His brow furrowed. "How much time you got?"

I let out an exasperated sigh as I glanced back at the screen. "Not enough for the situation I'm in—just a week. If I don't make it, I'll be front row center in the unemployment line."

His brooding expression softened.

"Yo, you hungry? Let's go grab something to eat," he suggested as he put on his boots. "Maybe it'll get your mind off it, at least for a little while."

I nodded, appreciative of the distraction. "Yeah, sure. That sounds good. Just let me freshen up."

About half an hour later, Dre led me outside to his sleek, black pickup truck. Relief washed over me. The exhilarating ride on the back of his motorcycle was terrifying, and I welcomed the change and the ability to blend in with everyday drivers. We climbed into the truck, and Dre started the engine.

As we drove, the engine's hum and the scenery passing by created a soothing backdrop. I glanced over at Dre; the glow of the afternoon sunlight illuminated his focused, melanated expression. He seemed so different when he wasn't trying to play the tough guy role—almost like a big teddy bear.

We approached the fast-food drive-through, and the familiar red neon sign came into view. He pulled up to the speaker and rolled down the window. Soon after, we were greeted by a cheerful voice.

"Welcome to Burger Palace. What can I get you today?"

He glanced over at me, arching a questioning brow. "You know whatchu want?"

I paused for a moment. "A cheeseburger and fries is fine. Oh, and a chocolate shake."

He nodded and turned back to the speaker. "Let me get a cheeseburger, seasoned fries, and a chocolate shake. And I'll also take a double bacon burger, large seasoned fries, and an orange soda."

After the drive-through attendant confirmed our order, Dre pulled forward to the window. As we waited, I felt a sense of normalcy warming my bones. The simplicity of the moment—relishing in the greasy comfort of cheeseburgers and seasoned fries—grounded me.

Our food arrived, and Dre handed me my shake and the greasy bag. I took a sip, savoring the sweet taste of the chocolate shake. We sat in his black pickup truck, parked in a quiet spot nearby, and started to enjoy our meals. I took a bite of my cheeseburger, thankful for the warm food, deliciously sweet shake, and his company. The trio provided a comforting change to all the danger we'd recently encountered.

We ate in comfortable silence until I was licking the salt off my fingertips, not realizing how hungry I was. As I sat there, letting my food digest, I relaxed. I wasn't ready to head back to the clubhouse.

"I think I want ice cream," I blurted out. "Can we grab some? I'm not ready to go back just yet."

"It'll start getting dark soon, Mercy. We really should be getting back."

"Just a little while longer, please?"

Dre nodded, finishing his burger. "Sure. I know a place."

He drove us to an ice cream shop in a secluded spot about an hour out of the city—a small park where the stars were visible through all the light pollution. Dre hopped out and laid out a blanket in the bed of his truck. I joined him.

"This place is beautiful. How'd you find it?"

"It's my hideaway. A place I come to whenever I need to think. I don't share it with anybody, but you looked like you needed to clear your head."

I smirked, appreciating the gesture. "You're damn right about that. Life is kicking my ass right now."

"What made you want to be a journalist anyway?" he probed.

I didn't know why his question surprised me.

"I've always loved telling real stories. But more than that, give a voice to the voiceless."

"Sounds personal."

"It kind of is."

Dre nodded with a look of respect in his eyes.

"That's wassup. Not too many people are willing to do that. Nowadays, it's all that microwave media shit—comes in fast and hot, then the next day, it's gone."

I nodded in agreement, appreciating his insight. "What about you? What made you join the Hell's Savages?"

Dre hesitated, then sighed.

"Family," he answered simply. "My father's the leader, and I'm his vice president. Besides that, it's all I've ever known. It's not always easy, but it's my life."

As we sat in the back of his black pickup truck, I felt an unexpected connection growing between us, understanding the pressures we both faced, although on opposite sides of the law.

"You said your father's your leader, right? What was it like growing up in a motorcycle club?"

He leaned back, staring at the sky as he considered his answer.

"There's a lot of loyalty, a lot of brotherhood. But there's also a lot of responsibility and pressure to live up to the club's expectations. My father's always been tough on me, but it's because he wants me to be strong."

"Ah, hence why you need a quiet place to come and clear your mind," I stated, concluding on my own. "You ever wish you could do something else?"

Dre chuckled, a dazzle of curiosity in his gray orbs. "Nah. The club is my family. I could never walk away from that."

"What's next for you in the club then? You're already the second in command. Any dreams or goals to take the throne?"

Dre shrugged his muscular shoulders.

"Honestly, I haven't thought much about it. I'm so focused on the here and now, making sure I'm doing right by my brothers and my father. But maybe one day, if it came down to it, I'd take the reins."

I leaned my head back against the truck's back window. The serenity of the moment calmed my nerves. I felt a pang of admiration for Dre, ready and willing to fill his father's shoes if and when the time came. At least he had set goals for himself. I didn't know what the fuck my plan B would be if I didn't keep my job.

I couldn't stop my thoughts from drifting back to the weight bearing down on my shoulders. The possibility of losing my career, not just my job, was the elephant in the room I couldn't disregard.

"What's next for you if you get fired?" Dre questioned as if he had the power to read my thoughts.

A loud sigh escaped my lips, my mind still racing with doubt.

My shoulders rose and fell. "I honestly don't know. My journalism career means everything to me. It's not just about the paycheck, y'know? If I lose it, I'll have no choice but to figure out a new path. Maybe I can do some freelance work while I try to find another permanent position. But it's fucking tough out there. Jobs in my field aren't that easy to come by."

Dre listened, his expression empathetic.

"I can tell you're passionate about what you do. Even if shit doesn't work out with your current job, I know you'll find another way to make an impact on the world."

"Thanks. I just gotta stay focused and pray everything works out for my good. This story is my chance to prove… a lot."

"To who?"

"To everybody. Myself included."

"Why? What's in it for you if all this goes public?"

I sighed, shoulders slumping as if I had anchors tied to my arms. "It's probably going to sound crazy."

"Try me."

"Secondhand justice."

His eyebrows pulled together. "What the fuck is secondhand justice?"

"Years ago, back when I was a sophomore in high school, I was sexually assaulted by my English teacher."

His jaw clenched. "I'm sorry to hear that."

I nodded. "Yeah. It was crazy. But the most fucked-up part is that I told the principal what happened to me, and nothing happened."

"Nothing?"

"Nothing," I confirmed. "He kept teaching, and probably kept touching other girls with no consequences. I learned years later that he was the principal's brother-in-law. The sick fuck was probably in on it all along. For once, I just want a hand in putting monsters like that in jail where the fuck they belong."

"What high school did you go to?"

"Grantville. Home of the Pelicans."

"What year did you graduate?"

"Two-thousand-eighteen, why?"

He looked away for a few seconds as if he were going back and forth with himself about something.

"What if I could get you something better than a witness?" he offered, bypassing my question. "Something that couldn't be denied or questioned."

My curiosity was instantly piqued, causing me to sit my head back up. "What's better than a crucial witness?"

His eyes met mine. "Video proof. If we can get footage of the Outlaws in action for your article, there's no way your boss or whoever can deny it. It's solid evidence that will force the police to get involved and put a stop to this shit."

My eyes widened, and hope rekindled in my gut. I had to stop myself from jumping up and hugging him. "Could you get me footage?"

Dre nodded slowly as if already working through the logistics in his mind.

"I have some contacts who might be able to help. I know you're on a deadline, but we can't rush this. We have to be careful."

I nodded eagerly. With his help, I could finally get the evidence I needed to expose the Outlaws and bring justice to the women they'd harmed. I looked at him and smiled. He wasn't just protecting me. He was helping to uncover the truth and bring down his enemies.

Unable to refrain myself, I reached out to hug him, crashing my body against his. "Thank you so much, Dre. I swear I'll make sure this story brings those creeps to justice."

"You're welcome," he replied, his hard chest still pressed against mine.

As I pulled away, I noticed Dre staring at me, his steely gray eyes full of blazing intensity.

"Why are you staring at me like that?" I quizzed, barely above a whisper.

He hesitated as a slow smirk lifted the corner of his lips. "Because I'm fighting the urge not to kiss your beautiful ass right now," he answered, voice gravelly.

My heart fluttered. "If it helps, you have my permission to stop fighting."

Dre leaned in, closing the distance between us. Our lips met in a gentle yet passionate kiss, sealing a moment of connection neither of us expected, but I suspected we both desperately needed.

———

It had been almost three days since our kiss under the stars, and there had been radio silence between us. I didn't know where Dre disappeared to. He was like a ghost. I found myself navigating life in the Hell's Savages clubhouse in his absence, slowly becoming acquainted with the club members around the clubhouse. The motorcycle club was nothing like I imagined. It was a different world and nothing like I thought it would be.

Over the past few days, I met several members who'd welcomed me in their own rough but genuine way. There was Blaze, the mechanic. He'd gone out with a few other men to bring my car back to the clubhouse and run a diagnostics test to find out what was wrong. Turns out I had a leaking head gasket. He scolded me for not taking it to a mechanic sooner. I admitted I didn't know the first thing about cars besides how to drive them and put gas in the tank. Luckily, I kept a gym bag in my trunk with a couple of spare outfits inside for emergencies.

Then there was Ghost—the enforcer. He had a no-nonsense attitude and was fiercely protective of his brothers. He talked to me about my work as a journalist, boasting that his younger sister was attending an HBCU and studying communications just like I did.

Lastly, there was the president, Dre's father. He was quiet but also incredibly calculated and forceful. He was the one who explained his club's code of honor to me, providing me with more insight into their MC family.

I found myself falling down the rabbit hole, slipping into Dre's world, and realizing the Hell's Savages were more than just a pack of rugged, ruthless criminals. They had a code, a fierce sense of loyalty, and an unwavering respect for justice that I'd quickly come to respect. I felt a strange sense of belonging among them.

Despite my growing comfort, I couldn't shake the thoughts of Dre. Our brief but intense connection still lingered in the back of my mind, slipping to the front at the most inopportune times. His abrupt disappearance had left me with a lot more unanswered questions than I could process. Did he regret our kiss? Was it so bad that he couldn't stand to be near me? We never talked about our past relationships. Maybe he had a girlfriend and felt guilty about what happened between us. The possibilities were endless.

*The next time I see him, I will make him talk to me about what happened and what the hell comes next.*

---

Later that night, the Hell's Savages were hosting one of their weekly MC parties. The clubhouse was alive and well with thumping rap music, laughter, MC groupies, and the clinking of shot glasses and beer cans. I found myself mingling with the members, enjoying the lively atmosphere. Blaze offered me a drink, and we started chatting about my car.

As we talked, I felt a sense of belonging I hadn't felt in a long time. I didn't have a close knit group of girlfriends I could call on at the drop of a dime just to shoot the shit. I wasn't kee-keeing in a group chat about something silly somebody posted online. I was a loner, and loners didn't make good friends, and definitely not consistent ones.

Our moment of harmless chatter was interrupted when Dre stormed over to us wearing a venomous expression.

"What the fuck are you doing out here? You're supposed to be in the room!" he barked, his voice booming like thunder over the music.

My eyes popped wide. I was half surprised, half pissed off. I'd had enough of being told what to do like I was a damn child.

"I'm not your fucking prisoner," I snapped. "You've been gone for days. You really couldn't have expected me to stay cooped up in that room forever like a pet in a cage."

The room fell silent, the other members watching our confrontation as if we were on a live reality TV show.

Dre grabbed my arm. "Come with me. Now."

He dragged me back to his room, his grip firm but not painful. Once inside, he released me, his eyes flaming with anger.

"Don't *ever* fuckin' embarrass me like that again."

My anger flared as I folded my arms across my chest. My breasts swelled with a lungful of air.

"I'm not a child, Dre! I can't just sit in this fucking room all day and twiddle my fucking thumbs. I need to breathe fresh air and interact socially with people. I can't live like a prisoner."

"I'm trying to protect you the best way I know how," he argued, voice getting louder.

I kept my arms folded, standing my ground. "By smothering me? You can't keep me locked up. I need to finish my story, Dre. My career depends on it. I've told you this a million times already."

He took a deep breath, visibly trying to control his anger. "I'm not trying to smother you, all right?"

"Then let me do something, *anything*. Contrary to what you think, I'm not made of glass, and I'm not some damsel in distress that needs saving all the time."

I couldn't take it anymore. The only way I'd clarify my point was to take my chances and leave. I stormed out of the room, slamming the door in my wake.

"Mercy, wait," Dre called out, chasing after me.

I didn't stop as my legs and anger propelled me forward. I burst out of the clubhouse and into the dimly lit parking lot. A frustrated ache prowled about my chest as he followed me.

"Mercy, stop! You can't just run off like this."

I spun around on my heels. "Watch me. I'm done being treated like a prisoner. I need to get the fuck out of here. Consider yourself off my protection detail, Mr. Bodyguard."

Dre reached out, grabbing my swinging arm to stop me.

"Hold up. You're not thinking straight. It's not safe out there."

I yanked my arm free, my eyes burning with defiance.

"I don't give a fuck. I'd rather take my chances out there than be trapped in here with you for one more second!"

Dre's handsome expression remained hardened, his frustration boiling over.

"Fine. Fuck it then. Go ahead and run. But don't come crying to me when you realize how dangerous it is with the Outlaws on your ass, Mercy, because I won't give a fuck," he promised.

I glared at him, my anger matching his. "I don't need you to save me, nigga. I can take care of myself."

The challenge hung in the air between us, fueling the tension already thick enough to cut a knife. Dre stepped back, his expression hardening before he unlocked his truck and walked around to slide into the driver's seat. He rolled down the window before I could storm off again and beckoned me to get in. I rolled my eyes, got in on the other side, and shut the heavy door with a loud thud.

"I don't even know why I got in the truck with you. You're the last person I want to see right now," I grumbled while snapping my seat belt in place.

"Yeah, well, I guess we're both out here doing shit we never do.

Because nothing in this world would *ever* make me want to chase after a woman."

"Then why the hell are you out here?"

"I wish I fuckin' knew," he grunted.

I didn't know everything about Dre, but I knew enough. I'd met men like him over my twenty-five years—overly possessive and mad at the world. He might've been five, maybe six years my senior, if that. He started the engine and peeled out of the clubhouse's parking lot, driving like a bat out of hell.

"Where the hell are we going?" I snapped.

"You said you wanted to leave, right? Sit the fuck back and shut up."

I scoffed before easing back into the passenger seat, feeling the cool leather against my skin.

I didn't reply immediately, focusing my attention on the road. His knuckles gripped the steering wheel. He turned his gaze to me, meeting my fiery eyes with a calm intensity after a moment of tense silence.

"You calm now?"

"Why do you care?"

"Because who the fuck else was going to make sure you're okay?"

I let out a short bark of bitter laughter. "Always playing the gallant white knight."

The teasing tone returned in his voice. "Only if you play the damsel in distress."

I shook my head. "Trust me, I'm over that."

Dre smirked. "Too bad. I've always had a thing for damsels."

Silence filled the car again. I studied him from the passenger seat, my eyes softening from their previous fire.

"Where are you taking me, Dre, really?"

Instead of answering, he pulled into the parking lot of a local park. It was so late that we were the only vehicle in the lot.

"Here. Happy now?" he quizzed, but there was no heat behind it.

I shrugged. "Maybe."

I bit my bottom lip and glared at him for a few moments. The surprise in his eyes was almost satisfying. *Almost.*

"I can't tell if you like me or hate me," I muttered.

He met my gaze and answered honestly. "You hate me, Mercy. I hate you back. That's our thing. I protect you. We bicker. I drive you up a wall."

"Yeah, you do. I'm starting to wonder why you do it so much, especially since you ghosted me after that kiss."

He choked on a laugh, his eyes widening in disbelief. "What? Nah. It wasn't like that… I mean you and me… it's not like that. You annoy the shit out of me," he stammered out, looking everywhere but at me.

I leaned back against my seat and watched him fumble his response. "Whatever. You can drop me off right here if you lured me into this truck to rub salt in my wound."

He chuckled lowly. "The last thing I came here to do was rub salt in your wound, Mercy. I drove you here to tend to it since no one else would."

I rolled my eyes. "As if you'd let them if they tried."

"You're probably right about that."

An unfamiliar heat replaced the tension in the truck. Both of us knew it wasn't hate sparking the flame.

"But for the record," Dre added, turning to face me fully, our bodies were mere inches apart in the confined space of his truck, "I don't hate you. You just rile me up and piss me off so bad I think I do."

I sighed heavily. "It's not on purpose. I'm just on ten right now. I feel like I'm trapped in a snow globe that keeps being turned upside down. I can't catch a damn break. Have you made any leads with the video footage?" I asked. "I only have a few more days to write my article."

"I don't want to talk about that right now. Honestly, I don't want to talk at all anymore."

"Then what do you wanna do?"

"You."

My heart thudded as Dre's confession hung in the air. The truth, simple, raw, and unfiltered, was finally revealed in the dim glow of the dashboard light. I felt it too. I wanted it. I wanted my body beneath his, my tongue silenced by deeper, sweeter sounds.

"I think I want that too," I replied, voice barely above a whisper.

"So, is that an invitation?" he questioned, his voice gravelly with want.

He was right there, just inches from me. It was the closest we'd been since the first and last time we kissed. I inhaled, drawing in the hypnotic scent of his cologne, mingling with the faint smell of leather from his seats.

"No. It's a demand," I said, fire burning bright in my eyes as I unbuckled my seat belt and turned to face him.

Dre was stunned into silence before a low chuckle rumbled from his chest. My breath hitched when he reached over to trap my chin gently between his thumb and forefinger, forcing me to meet his gaze head-on.

"You sure about this, Mercy? You sure you want to play with fire?"

"Never been more sure about anything," I confirmed. "And trust me, I can handle the heat."

The clock on the dashboard read one thirty-seven a.m., the glow illuminating his bearded face as he reached across the divide to place his hand on my thigh. The warmth of his big hand seeped through my skin, sending an electric current straight to my yoni.

"Mercy, I don't think you mean what you're saying. You're just all wound up because a nigga got you mad."

"I mean it, Dre," I retorted, my voice a husky growl. "I want you. One night. One time."

I needed to feel a release. I needed to feel the warmth of his tattooed body against mine. I needed to feel better inside and out.

"I hope you know what you're getting into," he warned me one final time.

His spare hand covered mine, squeezing gently before he turned off the truck. His mind was already made up.

*There's no turning back now. We're doing this.*

I unbuckled my jeans before gliding my hands up his abs. "I know exactly what I'm getting into," I replied as my lips quirked into a predatory smile that made my blood hum under my skin. "Now shut up and fuck me."

Dre placed his tattooed hand on my chest, his fingers tracing the outline of my collarbone through my T-shirt.

"So fuckin' bossy," he murmured, reaching over to my side and pulling me closer.

I giggled. "You know you love it," I retorted, my eyes never leaving his as I started tugging at his shirt's hem.

"And what if I do?" he asked, whispering in my ear.

I responded by capturing his lips in a searing kiss, my fingers tangling in his long locs as he groped blindly for my waist. The truck was an awkward place for sex, but I didn't care.

"Then prove it." I breathed against his lips once we finally broke apart for air.

And he intended to do just that.

With a swift motion, he managed to find the door handle, and we shuffled out and climbed into the back. Once again, he laid down the blanket, and we laid under the stars, my body hovering over his. The light from the streetlamp outside cast a soft glow on his face, accentuating his handsome features.

"Fuck, Mercy. You look so beautiful," Dre whispered, one hand sliding along the curve of my hip while the other braced against the side of the truck.

A devilish glint sparkled in my eyes at the sound of my name on his lips. It made me wet. I raised a challenging eyebrow and craned my neck. His mouth was hot against my pulse point.

"Show me how much you want to be inside me, Dre."

His animalistic instincts took over, and he captured my lips for another kiss, allowing the intensity between us to skyrocket. The heat engulfing us was intoxicating as we surrendered to our desires, letting pure passion dictate our actions.

Dre lifted my pink shirt, revealing my two perfect, mango-sized breasts. Not too small, but not too big. With urgency, he peeled off my shirt and bra, tossing them both to the side. My fingers traced patterns on his bare arms, each touch sparking a fire within him.

My nipples hardened under his gaze, a pure ash gray. My chest rose and fell with shallow breaths as he leaned in, his lips ghosting over my skin. My eyes fluttered closed, a soft sigh escaping my lips as he took one stiff nipple between his teeth.

I clutched his locs, pulling him closer as I arched into him.

"Dre," I gasped, my voice filled with such raw need that it only fueled the fire raging within me.

He trailed kisses along my collarbone as his fingers explored the warmth of my searing hot thighs, inching closer to where I needed him most. I bucked forward against his hand, begging for him to touch me. He started to peel down my jeans at the waist and my lace panties too. Shoes, jeans, and panties—I kicked them all off.

Naked, I shivered under his touch. My hand landed on his, guiding him where I wanted him to be.

I moaned. "Please," I begged, my voice hitching in anticipation.

Dre's fingers finally touched my wet heat, and I let out a strangled gasp. My body trembled under his touch as he dove into my world of sweet intoxication.

Leaning forward, he captured my lips in another heated kiss. It was a wild mix of teeth and tongue, hot breath mixed with soft sighs. My hand weaved through his locs, desperate to bring him closer despite the nonexistent space between us. With a hungry growl, he pressed himself against me, making me whimper with desire.

His hands were everywhere—tracing fiery trails over every inch of my exposed butterscotch skin. Rolling my clit with his calloused hands, he paid close attention to the pleasure dancing in my eyes. *Fuck.* I never thought I'd be craving to see him aching underneath me, yearning to be deep inside me.

Dre fumbled with his belt until he had his pants and boxer briefs down his legs, continuing to play with my clit along the way. He only stopped toying with me for a moment. It was long enough for me to hike up one of my legs and give him a deeper, wetter entry point. I looked down at him as he stared at my perfect pussy with the hunger of a man that couldn't wait any longer.

He lined himself up at my entrance, slapping his long, thick dick against my sopping-wet honeypot. I moaned as my hand reached down to guide him in.

I purred. "Ooh fuck, Dre."

He couldn't respond, lost in the tight sensation of pushing in and out of my silky warmth. Nothing had *ever* felt so fucking good.

My eyes cracked open the following morning, and I slowly turned my head to see Mercy sleeping naked and peacefully beside me in my bed. Her face was relaxed, her breathing steady, and her nipples were hard as diamonds under my gaze. For a moment, I just watched her, feeling a surge of lust and protectiveness wash over me. Thoughts of the night before danced in my head—her riding my dick under the stars in the back of my truck, the sweet serenade of her moans as she swallowed my nut.

Although I didn't want to admit it to myself or otherwise, Mercy had my nose wide open. If I was in the business of trying to give my heart away, hold hands, and whatever else lovey-dovey shit niggas did when Cupid shot them in the ass, I'd want it to be someone like Mercy. She had a smile that could give a thug butterflies, and the type of bark that made my dick throb.

I liked being with her. Better yet, I liked who I was when I was around her.

*I don't want anyone to even look at her. She's mine to protect.*

I felt confused, protective, and something deeper than I was ready to put a name on. I'd never felt this way about another woman before, and it scared the fuck out of me. I was used to being in control of my emotions, being able to turn them on and off with the flick of a switch, and falling in love with a gorgeous spitfire like Mercy was about as far out of control as I could get.

My relationships with women had always been complicated. I didn't kiss them. I didn't love them. And I damn sure didn't trust them. All I did was fuck them.

My trust issues were shaped early by the abandonment of my mother when I was a toddler. The only thing she left behind were a few pictures of us and a deep-rooted feeling of neglect and mistrust.

My father was strict with me growing up, demanding that I go the extra mile. Maybe he was tougher on me because I didn't have that nurturing maternal figure. I didn't know. But he always made sure that if I didn't know anything else, I knew the values of loyalty, something she knew nothing about.

I hated the fact that my mother chose to ditch her family and build a new life with another nigga and raise a new kid like she hadn't left one behind. It was a bitter fuckin' pill to swallow. So, I kept my guard up, fearing that any female I let in would eventually leave me, just like that bitch did.

Everything changed when I saw Mercy. I felt like a sucker for catching feelings for her so fuckin' quickly, but I couldn't deny the connection I felt with her. My internal mental struggles only added to my protectiveness over her and the difficulty I had in telling her how I felt. I wanted to keep her safe from the dangers of my dark world, but doing so meant leaning into the vulnerability that came with giving her my already broken heart.

Gently, I reached out and stroked her long, wavy hair that

shielded her right eye, my fingers brushing through the ebony strands. She stirred slightly but didn't wake up. My heart sprinted up to my throat.

*I'll keep my girl safe, come hell or high water.*

As I watched her sleep, I thought about the past few days—the arguments, the moments of connection, and our first kiss, and fucking under the stars. I knew we had a long road ahead, but I was willing to face whatever came our way. For her—only her.

I froze when Mercy stirred again. Her eyes fluttered open. She yawned and sat up, stretching her arms before realizing her supple breasts were exposed. I quickly looked away, feeling a mix of emotions, although I'd already seen her naked and buried my dick inside her.

"Good morning," she greeted with a lazy smile.

"Wassup. You must be hungry. I'll go out and bring back some food."

I stood up, ready to leave the room, but Mercy's sweet voice stopped me. "The only thing I'm hungry for is more of you."

I swung my head. "That's not what you said last night."

"I reserve the right to change my mind."

"You were the one who said one night, one time. I'm just trying to keep that same energy."

She scoffed. "Why are you acting different since we fucked?" she asked, pulling the covers over herself to cover her body.

I hesitated with my back still turned to her. I took a deep breath, trying to find the right words, before I finally turned to face her, my expression conflicted.

"Because you're too fuckin' innocent for this world, and I don't want to taint you."

Mercy's eyes widened in surprise and frustration.

"Taint me? I thought we talked about this last night, Dre. I'm not some fragile flower. I want more of this, especially with you. It doesn't have to be anything more than sex if that's what you're worried about."

"It's not."

"Then why are you pushing me away? I don't understand."

A strong surge of emotions coursed through me, my protective nature clashing with my growing feelings for her. I wanted to tell her the truth, but every time I thought about opening my mouth and letting the words come out, I couldn't bring myself to do it. I wasn't a vulnerable nigga. Feelings weren't my thing, but fucking was.

I sucked my teeth. "You're being stubborn as hell right now."

"How? Because I'm telling you I'm capable of taking care of myself? That I don't need you to protect me from everything?"

I sucked my teeth in frustration. The more she argued with me, the more I found myself holding back from doing the one thing I'd been wanting to do since I'd turned her mouth into a daycare the night before—dig that waterpark of a pussy out again.

"You know what, fuck this shit. On your knees," I barked, stepping forward as I undid my belt. "Since you don't wanna fuckin' listen."

One look in her eyes, and I knew her pussy was clenching in excitement. Still, she chose to defy me. "Excuse me?"

"You fuckin' heard me, Mercy."

"And if I don't? What are you gonna do, Dre? Punish me?"

"You goddamn right I am."

Mercy lowered her eyes only to look up through her long lashes before one side of her mouth lifted in a smirk. "Good."

I smirked back, leaning against the dresser with the belt in my hands. "Get on your knees."

She obliged, and I rewarded her with slight praise. "Good girl. Now bend forward and stick that ass in the fuckin' air. Five for disobedience, if you talk back, it's ten. Do you fuckin' understand?"

"Yes."

"Good."

I stepped closer, the leather of the belt making a loud 'swish' sound as it left my hand. I stood behind her, a hulking figure against her petite frame. Her nipples grew hard in anticipation.

"One," I said, and then there was a loud crack as the belt connected with her plump ass cheeks.

She gasped, feeling the sting where it connected. "Ouch! That hurt, Dre," Mercy cried out, immediately regretting talking back as pain shot through her.

"Two," I counted, not hesitating to follow up with another smack, this one even harder than the first. "Three."

"Four," she counted for me as another sharp slap echoed through the room.

I sent one more down, hard, and she bit her lip to keep from crying out.

"Now," I growled in her ear. "Spread your legs, and put your hands behind your back," I commanded and she did as told, her breath coming in short gasps as my warm hands skated down her spine. I smacked her ass again for good measure before pushing my erection deep inside of her from behind, filling her tight ass pussy completely.

"Fuck," I grunted, beginning a slow rhythm that had her hips bucking off the bed, desperate for release even though she was already wet and eager for me. Mercy moaned loudly as I took her hard and fast, tilting her hips up for deeper penetration whenever I allowed it.

The room began to spin around us. It was as though I was floating on a cloud with each thrust bringing me higher and higher. The sound of skin slapping against skin echoed through the room. Her body was tight and shaking with the signs of an incoming orgasm.

I grabbed her neck, squeezing until just before she couldn't breathe, making her eyes roll back into her head. My grip on her neck tightened as I leaned forward for a deep kiss, my tongue forcing its way into her mouth and battling with hers before biting down on her bottom lip.

Then, without warning, I pulled out before burying my face between her sticky thighs. Mercy's eyes rolled back into her head at the feeling—different from my dick but equally as pleasurable. I lapped at her throbbing clit like a starved man at a feast, sucking hard enough to make her see stars while my fingers danced inside of her, searching for that sweet spot that would send her soaring into orbit.

"Oh God," she cried out, arching off the bed as another wave of pleasure crashed over her. "Please... don't stop."

Her voice came out broken and needy, begging me for release even though I knew it wasn't time yet. And then I did something even more wicked, I bit down gently on her inner thigh, a punishment for running her fuckin' mouth so much. She moaned, and I knew I'd delivered the perfect blend of sting and pleasure.

Mercy exploded on my tongue, screaming out my name as wave after wave of orgasmic bliss washed over her. I lapped at her sweet nectar before coming up, my beard glistening with her cum. I couldn't help but grin.

"Good girl, let's see if we can go for number two. Turn around, ass in the air."

Mercy scrambled to obey, getting on her knees and arching her back just the way I liked. *How'd she know?*

Anticipation coursed through me as my hard length pressed against her entrance, teasingly brushing against her opening but never quite penetrating.

"Please, Dre," she whined, "I need you deep inside me."

I chuckled darkly. "I will be," I promised, pulling back before slamming into her with a groan. This time it was different—rawer, rougher, harder. My nails bit into her hips and I began to pound into her without mercy, grunting with each thrust as I knocked the bottom out of her pussy.

"Is this what you wanted? Huh? Is this what the fuck your ass was whining for?" I growled.

She moaned. "Yes! Yes! Don't stop!"

I heard the headboard repeatedly hitting the wall in front of us with each impact as Mercy's sweet lips formed an 'o' of shock. Her eyes rolled back into her head again as another orgasm crashed over her.

My hand twisted around her hair, yanking her head back as the curve of my dick hit her G-spot again and again. "Cum for me again, baby girl, and I'll give you anything you want."

With a whimpering cry, Mercy's next climax began to build once more. My grip on her hair tightened, my rhythm relentless as I continued to pound into her pussy, eager to send her careening over the edge. She clawed at the sheets beneath her, desperate for something to hold on to as the waves of ecstasy crashed over her.

"Yes!" she screamed. "Oh God, yes!" Mercy's back arched even further as her next orgasm tore through her body like a California wildfire, more intense than the first. Her body twitched as her core contracted around my thick length.

"Fuck!" I growled, my body tense and shaking as I spilled my seed inside her moments later.

As her cries faded, Mercy collapsed onto the bed, boneless and spent. I withdrew from her and pulled up my jeans.

"If you don't want my protection, fine. You're without it," I growled before leaving the room, hearing the door slam behind me.

I sat in my truck, seething and gripping the steering wheel so tight I thought I'd break it in two. I was more pissed off with myself than anything. I couldn't tell Mercy how I felt about her to her face. It felt too soon, too damn intense. Given how quickly everything unfolded between us, I worried she'd think it was weird. Frustrated, I decided to swallow my feelings and sit on them in the meantime, thoughts drifting to my time away from her.

The three days I was gone hadn't been in vain. I'd been handling business and ensuring I lived up to my club name and raised pure Hell when it came to Mercy's high school English teacher and principal.

As soon as I found out about what happened to Mercy, I put one of the prospects who specialized in tech and computer shit on researching their names. Within hours, he found a digital yearbook online to get their names, then cross-referenced them with DMV records to find their addresses.

I wasted no time running down on them one at a time, starting with the principal. He was supposed to be her protector, the one she went to for help at school when something went wrong. Instead, he'd chosen to side with a pedophile. I didn't fuck with that.

I sat in the back seat of his car watching him kiss his doting wife goodbye at the doorway at seven-thirty in the morning. He turned on his heels, certain he'd have the same day he'd always have. Until he met me. As soon as his ass hit the cloth driver's seat, his eyes met my grimaced reflection in his rearview mirror. My gloved hands were around his throat before his bitch ass had a chance to scream.

*Snap.*

With one quick twist, his neck was broken and he was dead.

*One down, one to go.*

I saved Mr. Hubertson, the English teacher, for last. I let him get through the entire school day, wanted to make him feel that nothing in his sick, perverted little life was out of order. Until that fuckin' bell rang. Then, his ass was mine.

I waited until he walked out to his car after school and confronted him in the parking lot. He tried to run from me when I asked him if he liked touching lil girls more than he liked teaching mothafuckas how to read. I slammed him back on the pavement, head-first of course. He didn't move much after that. I pulled out my Glock, wrapped my gun around his hand, and put it up to his head before pulling the trigger and watching his brains splatter. I hopped on the back of my bike and peeled off.

I had the blood of two more men on my hands for Mercy, but if that meant she never had to worry about them hurting anyone ever again, I'd do it again.

My thoughts stirred with the buzz of my cell phone in my pocket. I fished it out and looked at the screen to see a blocked number. My eyes shifted from left to right before I pressed accept and pressed the phone tightly to my ear.

"Speak."

"I have the footage you asked for," Rex, my inside man with the Outlaws, informed me. "When can you meet?"

"Give me a location, and I'm on my way."

"I'll text you. Meet me in twenty."

"Bet," I replied before ending the call.

My heart somersaulted in my chest. As indifferent as I was about my feelings for Mercy, I still wanted to do everything I could to help her win.

After receiving the flash drive from Rex twenty minutes later, I couldn't wait to get back to Mercy and present it to her. I knew whatever doubts she had about me would dissipate as soon as she had the drive in her possession. Unable to get her off my mind, I realized I'd made a mistake in telling Mercy she no longer had my protection. I was just talking out the side of my fucking neck. I never meant that shit. I wanted to be with her, and I was a fool for walking away.

My foot tapped the gas a little harder, desperate to get back to her side. I turned down a secluded back road, when I noticed something in my rearview mirror. A group of bikers were following me and closing in fast. My heart rate gunned into overdrive as I recognized the Chicago Outlaws MC patches.

*Fuck. Not now.*

Before I could react, they surrounded my truck, forcing me to pull over. I quickly hid the drive in my glove compartment. The bikers dismounted, their faces hidden by helmets and masks. My hand instinctively moved to my gun concealed underneath my seat, but it was too late. They yanked open the door and dragged me out, overpowering me in number and muscle. Suddenly, I felt a sharp pain in the back of my head, and everything started to fade to black.

They roughly threw me into the back seat of my truck, the impact jarring my already aching head. They sped off, the rumble of motorcycles following close behind. I struggled, feeling the vibrations of the road beneath me. Thoughts of escape raced through my head, but there was no evading the hood over my head and the zip ties clasped tightly around my wrists.

"Got him. Good work, Rex. Let's move," Cannon announced.

As they sped away, my mind galloped with alarm. I knew the Outlaws had taken me for a reason, and it wouldn't be a pleasant reunion.

———

After what felt like a decade, the truck came to a halt. I heard the doors open and the thudding sound of approaching footsteps. They pulled me out of the truck and yanked the hood off my head. Before I could react, what felt like a steel-plated fist connected with my jaw, sending a fresh roll of ache rolling through my body.

I blinked against the lighting as the faces of my captors started to come into focus—members of the Outlaws. Cannon stepped forward. I squirmed, but a punch to my ribs made me double over in pain.

"Thought you could fuck with us and get away with it, mothafucka?"

I glared at him, refusing to show any fear. "You fucked up taking me. My brothers will find out what you did and come for me."

Cannon barked out a cruel laugh. "And all this time, I thought I was your brother."

"You could never be a brother to me, nigga," I spat. "The Savages are my family."

"By the time they find you, you'll be in pieces, nigga," he warned.

I knew the Savages would be looking for me, but I had to hold out until the cavalry arrived. The aches in my ribs and jaw were intense, but I centered my thoughts around my survival, determined not to give the Outlaws the pleasure of seeing me break down, especially not fuckin' Cannon.

"Y'know, I could make this end right now if you just give me what I want."

I glared at him, feeling the blood running down my face, and still refusing to show any sign of weakness.

I grunted. "Eat a dick, nigga. I'm not giving you shit."

Cannon leaned in closer. "Oh, come on. We both know you're holding onto that pretty lil journalist. What was her name again? Mercy? Tell me where she is, and I'll let you go."

My heart was jackhammering at the sound of her name, but my mind was made up. I couldn't let Mercy fall into his fuckin' hands.

"You'll never get her, so you may as well do your fuckin' worst to me," I growled, ready to take every blow to protect her.

Cannon's cruel, twisted smile faded, replaced by an irritated expression.

"You're willing to suffer for her, nigga? To die for a bitch you barely fuckin' know?"

I met his gaze, ensuring he saw the grit in my eyes. "I'll do *whatever* it takes to keep her safe."

He scoffed before delivering another punch to my ribs. A stinging throb shot through my body, but I gritted my teeth, refusing to fold.

"You're a fool, nigga. She's just some bitch. She ain't worth all this."

My mind flashed with pictures of Mercy—her smile, her laughter, the way her body felt wrapped around mine. I knew he was wrong.

"She's worth everything, nigga."

Cannon shook his head in disbelief, clearly frustrated by my strength. "We'll see if you'll be singing that same tune when you're coughing up blood," he growled.

I PACED AROUND Dre's bedroom, my anger simmering below the surface. I didn't like how easy it was for him to get under my skin, and I was pissed at him for storming out the way he did. Maybe I shouldn't have yelled at him like that. But he was so damn infuriating sometimes it was hard to breathe. Why couldn't he see I wasn't some fragile baby bird that needed protecting? I wasn't his forever problem. Our situation was temporary, wasn't it?

Despite my anger, I couldn't ignore the pull I felt toward Dre. The intensity of our arguments, not to mention the finger-lickin' good sex, only seemed to make me want him more. Emotionally, I was a crumpled-up mess of confusion and frustration. I didn't know why I felt anything for him. He was stubborn as a mule, overbearing as hell, and he didn't listen for shit. But he was also gallant and strong, and he looked at me like I was the only person in the world that mattered to him. Just picturing his warm gaze made my heart stutter. I'd fallen for a few wrong men in the past, but I'd never felt this way about anyone before, especially not so quickly.

As the hours ticked by, Dre hadn't returned, and my thoughts began to shift. I sat on the edge of the bed, replaying our argument in my head. *Maybe I overreacted.* Most women would've killed to have a man who was as fiercely overprotective of them as Dre was of me.

The more I thought about it, the more I realized my aggravation with him was rooted in uneasiness—the fear of my heart being unguarded, having to rely on someone other than myself, and the depth of my own adoration for him.

After what happened to me in high school, I always thought a part of me would never be whole again. But when I met Dre, he started to fill it. Before him, I thought it wasn't possible for anyone, including myself, to keep me safe. He'd proven that to be false.

I needed to talk to him. I had to apologize and explain how I felt. Maybe then we'd be able to find a level playing field. Determined to find him and settle the smoke between us, I showered, dressed, and headed toward the door. Admitting my feelings for Dre wouldn't be easy, but it was a step I had to take.

I searched the clubhouse, asking a few members if they'd seen him—no one had. I grew even more concerned when I headed outside and saw his black pickup truck was gone. My anxiety heightened as I headed to Dre's father's office, hoping he might've had some answers. I knocked on the heavy office door and heard him mumble for me to come in.

"Hi. I don't mean to bother you. I was wondering if you've seen Dre. We… uh, we argued earlier, and he stormed off. No one has seen him, and I'm getting worried about him."

He looked at me with a knowing expression before stroking his trimmed salt-and-pepper beard. "Give him some time to clear his head, Mercy. I'm sure he'll turn up soon. In the meantime, close the door. I can tell there's something else on your mind."

I nodded, gave him a once-over, and took my seat. He had to have been in his mid-to-late fifties and still had a commanding presence—the kind that demanded respect. He was tall and solidly built. It was easy for me to see where Dre got his brawny physique from. That, and his love for tattoos. His father's arms were covered in them too.

His salt-and-pepper hair was cut short, and his beard was freshly groomed. Despite the signs of aging around the corners, his eyes were still a sharp, penetrating brown that seemed to see right through me.

He sat behind his large desk wearing a leather vest adorned with the Hell's Savages' crest, over a simple black T-shirt that hugged his broad shoulders and muscular frame. I was sure he had on a pair of worn jeans and the heavy biker boots he always wore whenever I ran into him.

I took a deep breath, gathering my thoughts and emotions.

"Thank you for your hospitality, but I can't keep staying here. Blaze told me my car is fixed, and with Dre running off... I don't know. It feels like a sign that I should go."

He listened carefully before responding. "I appreciate your honesty. And I can see that you care about my son. But Dre's... complicated."

I sighed, a wave of frustration mingling with my anxiety.

"I've gathered that over the past few days. It's wild because I feel a pull toward Dre that I've never felt before. He's different, and despite all the chaos, I feel a strong connection to him. But maybe things aren't as meant to be as my head leads me to believe," I confessed, spilling my guts. "I wanna find him, but I don't know where to start. And if he's run off, maybe it's better if I leave too."

A sadness flickered in his eyes before he looked away, mentally wrestling with his decision on what to say next.

"My son isn't running from you, Mercy. He's running from his feelings. His mother left us when he was just two years old. She abandoned him and went to be with another man to live another life and even had another son. That son is now the head of the Outlaws MC," he revealed.

My eyes ballooned in shock. "Wait. You're telling me that the president of your rivals is his half-brother?"

I recalled our initial conversation when I asked him to give me information. *Fuck. That's why he didn't want to snitch.* Their rivalry went beyond the typical MC turf wars; it was deeply fucking personal. He probably saw his half-brother as a walking, breathing symbol of his mother's betrayal. But still, they were family.

"Yes," he confirmed. "Dre has always had a hard time forming attachments with women. He's afraid of being abandoned, of being hurt again. But I can see that he cares about you. It's why he's so protective. The fact that he's gone out of his way to take care of you means something. I don't think he wants to lose you. But if you want to leave, I won't stop you. But know that you've made an impression on him and all of us here."

A rush of emotions consumed me. I sympathized with Dre and better understood what made him tick. I cared about him more than I realized. But I didn't know how to save him if he couldn't face his feelings.

"Thank you. I do like him a lot. I know it's fast, but he makes me feel safer than I've ever felt before. I was scared to admit it at first, but now… I don't know what I'd do without him."

His father leaned forward. His brown-eyed gaze was reassuring.

"You've got spunk, Mercy. I'll give you that. I can see why my son is drawn to you. I'll try calling him. Maybe he just needs to hear your voice to set his ass straight."

I nodded hopefully as he picked up his phone and dialed Dre's number. After a few rings, someone answered, but from the sound of their voice, it wasn't Dre.

The harsh voice on the other line belonged to his half-brother, Cannon, the president of the Outlaws and the monster from my nightmare.

"Well, well. Looks like you're just in time for our family reunion," he taunted through the receiver. "We got your boy."

Fear clawed at my throat as anxiety burned a trail to my heart.

His father's grip on the phone tightened. "Where the fuck is my son, Cannon?"

"You know what we want. Hand over the reporter bitch, and we can talk terms."

"We both know that's not going to happen. I won't trade an innocent woman for my son."

Cannon laughed coldly. "Innocent? I found that bitch's badge the night she wandered into my bar. The bitch is a fuckin' journalist, poking her nose where it doesn't belong. She's a threat that needs to be eliminated one way or another. This is the deal, mothafucka. Take it or leave it."

My heart jerked against its tethers. *Oh shit. He knows I'm onto them.*

"If you harm my son, there will be hell to pay. You're already down men, Cannon. Let's be diplomatic and find another way to settle this."

His baritone voice deepened, taking on an even more menacing tone. "You've got twenty-four fuckin' hours to change your mind. After that, your baby boy won't be in one piece when you get him back," he warned.

The call ended abruptly—those three beeps before the line went dead. His father slammed the phone down, and I looked at him with fear dancing in my eyes.

"Oh my God. I... I'm so sorry. This is all my fault. W-what do we do now?"

His father's face was hardened with rage, but his expression softened slightly when he looked at me.

"It's not your fault," he assured me. "We'll find a way to get him back, but I won't let him lose you in the process."

The word of Dre's kidnapping swept through the Savages like a tornado. The clubhouse was in a frenzy as the members scurried to gather their weapons and mount their bikes to come to his aid. A knot of anxiety tightened in my throat. I knew the Outlaws were ruthless monsters, and the thought of them having Dre in their clutches made me nauseous.

Dre's father barked orders, his voice echoing through the clubhouse. His expression and tone remained stern when his eyes landed back on me.

"Mercy, you need to stay here. We can't risk you being out in the open."

Before I could protest, two prospects stepped forward, ready to escort me back to Dre's bedroom.

"But I want to help! I can't just sit here and do nothing while he's out there enduring God knows what."

One of the prospects shook his head, his expression sympathetic but firm. "Boss's orders. Let's go."

My heart dropped as they led me back to Dre's room. A wave of helplessness washed over me when I heard the door close behind me. I wanted to be out there, helping them find Dre, but instead, I was confined to his bedroom like a princess locked away in a tall tower.

I paced back and forth, every thought in my mind dashing with worry. The thought of Dre—the man I'd fallen for—enduring pain and suffering on my account was hard to swallow.

*This is all my fault. If I hadn't gone into that fucking bar, Dre wouldn't be in this mess.*

I flopped down on the edge of the bed, my hands quivering with worry. I'd never felt so tiny and powerless, and I couldn't stand it. I heard the muffled voices of the prospects standing guard outside the door. Their intimidating presence was a constant reminder of my quarantine.

I buried my face in my hands, trying to hide my tears. The fear and guilt gnawing at my gut were overwhelming, but I knew I had no choice but to keep my thoughts positive and believe that Dre would make it back to me in one piece.

I was bound to a metal chair in the center of the room, my body battered and bruised from the relentless beating. With my hands tied behind my back, I was defenseless. The tight zip ties pressed against my skin, adding to my discomfort.

The chair was anchored to the floor, preventing any chance of escape from the grim warehouse I was in. The building's walls were crumbling and covered in aged graffiti. The metal beams were rusted, and the air smelled of oil and decay. The concrete floor beneath my boots was stained with oil spills, broken glass, and scattered spare metal parts.

The Outlaws swarmed around me with their mugs hidden by their helmets. They were armed with their trigger fingers at the ready. In front of me stood Cannon, my younger half-brother and the leader of the Outlaws MC. A cruel smile played on his lips.

"Your father is on his way. And if he doesn't hand over that reporter bitch, I'm going to make my boys hold your eyes open and force you to watch while I kill him right in front of you."

I glared up at him, refusing to show any sign of weakness. Like me, Cannon had the same steely gray eyes. It was as if I was looking in the mirror. It was the only similar feature we shared. That, and an athletic physique. He sported a clean fade and a trimmed goatee.

Whenever I looked at him, I saw what my mother chose over me and the life I could've had. But I'd be damned if I let that affect my loyalty to my family and my vow to protect Mercy. I knew he was trying to break me, but I wouldn't give his ass the satisfaction. I was going to stay strong for myself and her.

"Tell me what you know about the article that bitch is working on."

I clenched my jaw, refusing to answer him. His smirk faded, replaced by a furrowed brow. He delivered another brutal blow to my ribs, causing me to grind my teeth in pain.

"Speak, mothafucka!"

I remained silent, my mind made up.

His eyes narrowed to a slit as he leaned in closer, his deep voice dripping with hate.

"You know, I can't wait to do unspeakable things to that pretty little bitch when I get her back. She's quite the beauty. Maybe I'll have some fun with her before I hand her over to the highest fuckin' bidder."

My blood boiled at the thought. My heart startled to a gallop just hearing that mothafucka speak her name. I couldn't stand anyone talking shit about Mercy. Not in my presence. The idea of her being harmed made my anger bloom.

"Touch her, and fuckin' I'll kill you," I growled.

He laughed, amused by my threat. "Oh, you've still got some

fight left in you, big bro? Good. It'll make this a lot more interesting."

"How many times I gotta tell your ass, you ain't no fuckin' brother of mine," I spat.

Cannon didn't care. He continued to taunt and beat me, but my thoughts stayed locked on two things: ensuring Mercy's safety and making it out alive so I could get back to her and tell her how I felt. She'd stolen a piece of me, and I wasn't taking it back.

Soon enough, I was barely conscious, my body aching from the relentless beating. With my eyes closed, I heard the distant roar of motorcycles and the unmistakable sound of gunfire. My heart galloped in my chest, throbbing recklessly. *It has to be them.* My father and the Savages had arrived.

Within seconds, the warehouse erupted into mayhem as the Savages clashed with the Outlaws head-on. Bullets zoomed through the air, evident signs of battle. My vision was blurred, but I struggled to stay alert. Amid the chaos I was engulfed in, I made out the blurred figures of my father and brothers fighting to rescue me.

"Hang in there, Son. We're getting you the fuck out of here," my father muttered when he reached me, his voice strained.

My brothers, the Savages, managed to overpower the Outlaws and free me from my binds. They carried me to the back seat of my pickup truck. I still felt the adrenaline of the fight running rampant through my veins. They had to stop me from going back in there and killing something.

As we sped away from the warehouse, my father's body was slumped over in the back seat, and his breathing was labored. I watched him with growing concern, noticing he'd taken a bullet in the side.

"Prez, you've been shot. We gotta get you to a hospital," I urged.

He swung his head, his voice weak but decided. "No time for

that, Son. Listen to me. You're going to lead the club now. And you need a good woman by your side. Mercy cares about you. Promise me you'll make things right with her."

His words pinched tears from my heart as I listened to my father's words, mentally recording them. "I will, Dad. I promise."

His eyes closed, and I felt him fading away. "I'm proud of you, Dreyson. Always have been."

With those final three words, I watched my father take his last breath in my arms. I howled out in pain, my heart shattering in ways I didn't know were possible. It had always been hard for me to shed a tear, but I couldn't do anything except cry like a newborn baby, my sobs wracking my tired body.

The Savages drove toward the clubhouse in silence, feeling the weight of our unimaginable grief tear through us like a tornado. After I helped lift my father's still body out of the back seat, I suddenly remembered something. I reached into the glove compartment and retrieved a flash drive. It was the video evidence I'd promised Mercy—surveillance proof of the Outlaws' involvement in illegally trafficking women. I shoved it into my pocket, vowing to honor my father's legacy, lead the club, and make things right with Mercy.

LEFT. *Right.*

*Left. Right.*

I paced back and forth in Dre's room for over an hour, my anxiety gnawing at my insides. The armed prospect stationed outside the door only added to my frustration. He wouldn't open the door, and he wouldn't tell me shit every time I begged for updates. The silence was agonizing.

Suddenly, I heard the rumbling of motorcycles in the distance. My heart tried to beat its way through my ribcage. Moments later, Dre burst through the door, bloody and beaten. I gasped, rushing straight to his side.

"Dre! Oh my God, are you okay?"

"I'm okay," he answered with a grunt, hand never leaving his ribs.

"You don't look it," I said, noting the pained expression on his bloodied face and bloodstains on his ripped clothes.

The club's medic, Doc, immediately rushed in with his medical supplies to tend to Dre's wounds—lacerations and bruised ribs. I remained close, holding his hand while Doc bandaged him and administered pain medication for comfort. My eyes never left his battered face.

"What happened, Dre? What did they do to you?"

He took a deep breath, quickly wincing from the pain before he recounted the ambush, the beatings, and the brawl that popped off when the Hell's Savages came to rescue him.

"I'm so glad you're okay. But—where's your father?"

He looked down, his voice growing quieter. "My father... he didn't make it, Mercy. He's dead."

My heart broke for him as tears welled up in the corners of my eyes. I wrapped my arms around him, unsure of what else to do. If I had the power to bring his father back, I would've.

"Oh, I'm so sorry, Dre." I looked at him, noticing the absence of tears in his eyes. "It's okay to cry. Let it out."

His voice was hoarse, filled with raw emotion. "I already did. I cried like a baby when he died in my arms. Now, I have to stay strong."

Reaching into his pocket, Dre pulled out a flash drive and handed it to me. "Here. This is the video evidence I promised you— proof of the Outlaws' sex trafficking. You need to leave while you can, Mercy. Cannon isn't dead, and I can't risk him coming after you. I'll have one of the prospects follow you wherever you need to go. I'll give you money, whatever you need."

I swung my head firmly. I refused to let him push me away.

"No, Dre. I'm staying right here with you. You're all I want."

Dre looked at me before pulling me close. He held me tight, and I knew we could face whatever came next together.

"I'm sorry for storming out on you the way I did. I was just caught up in my feelings for you, both good and bad. Still, I never should've left you, especially not without telling you how I feel about you. I've been holding back for fear of not wanting to scare you off, but if life has taught me anything today, it's the cruel lesson that time waits for no one. And I don't want to let another second go by without telling you how much I love you, Mercy Harris."

"I didn't think it would feel that good to hear you say that."

"Well, believe it, because it's the truth."

I leaned into him and gently pecked his lips before I whispered, "I love you too."

———

After hours of pouring through the videos and the intense work on my article, I finally submitted it to Mr. Charles, along with the video proof Dre had given me. The videos on the flash drive were damning—showing the faces, locations, and transactions of the Chicago Outlaws MC trafficking women. There was footage of them transporting terrified young girls in the back of trucks swarmed with motorcycles and handing them over to shady figures for money. Everything had been captured secretly by Dre and a few members of the Hell's Savages working on a secret task at the order of his father. It was undeniable and would surely blow the lid off the Outlaws' criminal operations.

Meeting my deadline *and* saving my job lifted a massive weight off my shoulders. Feeling exhausted but accomplished, I stepped out of the shower. The warm water washed away the stress of the day. I wrapped a towel around my dripping wet body and proceeded into the bedroom. It was after four in the morning when I crept over to my side of his bed and dropped my towel. I fully expected him to be asleep.

However, when I crawled into bed, I saw his eyes open, watching me intently.

"Did you finish your article?" he asked, voice groggy.

I nodded. "Yeah. I did. It's submitted, videos and all."

I caught a glimpse of Dre's weak smile through the sliver of moonlight peeking through the curtains. I buried my naked body under the covers and cuddled next to him, our skin touching. Feeling the warmth of his body against mine was as comforting as a warm blanket on a cold day.

I let out a deep sigh. "I'm so glad you're safe, Dre. I swear I don't know what I'd do without you."

He slowly wrapped his arm around me, wincing but still holding me close despite the discomfort it caused him.

"You're not getting rid of me that easily, woman. You're mine now."

I nodded, knowing I didn't want to belong to anyone else. As we lay there, I was sure what I'd said back to him earlier was true. I'd fallen in love with him. The zinging intensity of my feelings surprised me—hell, it even scared me—but that was how I knew it was real. I studied him, watching his eyelids flutter closed and his tatted chest's steady rise and fall.

Leaning in, I whispered, "I love you."

To my shock, he mumbled a response, his voice barely audible but the three words unmistakable.

"Love you too."

My heart froze mid-thump, shocked that he'd heard me. A warm smile spread across my face as I nestled against the pillow. For the first time in years, I was at peace.

———

*Three weeks later.*

The vibe inside the Hell's Savages' clubhouse was electrifying. The party had been raging since it started. We were all gathered there to celebrate Dre's recovery and the victory over the Outlaws, thanks to the publishing of my article. The somberness of recent events—losing and burying their president—was still fresh in our minds and hearts. For the first time in what felt like forever, the clubhouse was filled with laughter, music, and the celebratory clinking of champagne glasses and beer cans alike.

My investigative journalism skills, backed by the video evidence Dre provided, exposed the Chicago Outlaws MC for what they were—creeps on wheels, making their illegal activities undeniable. My article drew immediate attention from local and federal law enforcement agencies, who had been investigating the Outlaws but lacked the concrete evidence to make arrests.

I stood by the bar, a margarita glued to my hand, watching Dre make his rounds, mingling with his crew. He looked healthier, with the bruises and cuts mostly healed, though the emotional scars of losing his father remained. I took the last sip of my drink before licking my lips, keeping my eyes on the prize—Dre. I wanted him. Maybe it was the tequila. Perhaps it was the connection we both felt, but whatever it was, I wanted him bad.

I should've been having fun, tossing back shots with his crew, but all I could think about was feeling him buried deep inside me. We hadn't fucked since that night in his room, and my body was crying out for more. I'd had so many flashbacks to our sessions in the truck and on the bed, and the alcohol in my system only fueled my desire even more. My pussy was wet with need, and I was already five margaritas in.

Dre caught my eye from across the room. His eyes were steely gray, dark and inviting. He grinned at me, teeth white against his sweet brown skin and full of the promise of sinful pleasure. I put my margarita glass on the bar, watching him move toward me purposefully. His eyes never left mine, darkening further as he sauntered closer, heat radiating from every pore.

He stopped close enough for me to smell his smoky, masculine scent. Yet, he was far enough away not to touch but close enough to feel the heat rolling off him in waves.

"Enjoying your party?" I asked.

There was a playful grin on his handsome face. "I am now that I'm back over here with you."

"Good."

"Need a refill?" he queried in that velvety voice that sent chills down my spine.

"Not what I'm thirsty for," I replied huskily, biting my lower lip.

Dre turned to face me, and the air between us thickened with desire as the seconds flew by. He tilted his head to the side, signaling we should move to a quieter space. We walked away from the group, fingers laced together, as the noise of the party faded into the background. We headed toward the other side of the clubhouse, where most of the bikes and vehicles were parked. My car was located next to a shed. Instinctively, I walked around to the front and popped the hood.

"Open it up," he encouraged, his voice a low rumble that shot a thrill straight through me.

I flipped the latch and lifted the hood, leaning over the engine as if I knew what I was doing. *Perfect.* If anyone came up and saw us, they'd think we had to go into the shed to get something—oil, windshield wiper fluid, or something like it. I didn't care. I was prepared to do *whatever* to get his calloused hands running over my silky brown skin.

His hands came to rest on the edge of the hood, one on either side of me, as he moved in closer—so close I felt the warmth radiating from his body.

"Y'know, I never got to properly thank you for everything," he stated, his mouth a mere breath away from my ear.

The rumble of his voice against my skin sent pulses of heat down my spine. I smiled, feeling a familiar warmth spread through me.

"You don't have to thank me."

"I'm serious," he replied as his fingertips skated down my spine. "You stuck by me while I healed, while I buried my father. Plus, you stuck to your guns and finished your article. I'm in awe of you, Mercy. The way I feel about it has my insides all fucked up. It's fast, and it's twisted. It's everything it shouldn't be."

"Just because it's fast doesn't mean it's not right," I interjected. "I know it's been a crazy few weeks, but I know one thing for sure —I don't want to lose you, Dre."

My heart gave a kick, my feelings for him stronger than ever.

"You'll never lose me. I'm right here, ten toes down, and I'm not going anywhere," he confirmed.

Dre's gaze was molten, matching the fire I felt building inside me. I saw something flicker behind his eyes. Then, without warning, his lips were on mine—hot and deliciously demanding.

He snaked an arm around my waist, pulling me against him. His touch sent shivers through me as he slowly pulled away. His other hand brushed a loose strand of hair from my face before tucking it behind my ear.

I ran a hand along his chest as a smirk lifted the corner of my lip. "Is it wrong that I want you so bad right now?"

I dropped my gaze down to the bulge behind the pair of dark jeans he wore. His body language promised a night of sinful pleasure.

"You sure you want it here? Because if I start, I won't be able to stop," he warned in between kisses, his voice rough and husky. "I won't be able to control myself once I'm deep inside you, Mercy."

"Who says I want you to?" I replied teasingly, pulling away slightly to look into his smoldering eyes. His grip on me tightened. "Maybe I want you to ravage this pussy like only you can."

Dre sucked in a deep breath while his eyes were locked onto mine. He took my hand and pulled me around the other side of the shed—entirely out of view from the clubhouse.

There was a brief moment before he crashed his lips against mine again. There was so much savagery and passion that I wasn't the only one who felt the sexual connection the two of us shared.

Dre growled low in his throat as he pressed me up against the shed wall. The rough texture scraped against my back, making me gasp into his mouth. He took the opportunity to sweep his tongue inside, tasting me, claiming me.

His calloused hands roamed over my body as if he couldn't get enough of touching me. His fingertips traced the curve of my hips, my waist, up to the swell of my breasts. I gasped again at the pure, raw sensation of it all—his lips on mine, the way his body pressed into me. I was drowning in an ocean of desire, and it was all because of him.

"I haven't been able to stop thinkin' about that pussy of yours," he admitted between ragged breaths, his eyes blazing even brighter than before. "You have no idea how much I want it."

There was a tone to his voice that made my knees turn to water —a desperate longing that matched my own. My fingers remained curled around his bulge, rubbing his hard dick through his jeans.

*God, I want to taste him.* I wanted to know if I could fit his thick dick down my throat. His elephant trunk filled me up so much the last time we were together, and I felt him for days after—a lovely reminder of the sex we had, which was why I wanted it so bad the morning after.

"Probably as much as I want this," I replied, squeezing his dick before dropping to my knees.

Dre grabbed a fistful of my hair in his hand as I unbuckled his belt, pulled his zipper down, and freed his brick-hard rod.

I took as much of him in my hand as possible and stroked him slowly. His dick twitched as I circled my thumb around the leaking tip, spreading the bead of pre-cum. Dre grunted in approval, and his grip tightened around my hair.

"Look at you taking control," he said, voice laced with raw need. "You look so fuckin' good on your knees for me."

His dirty talk sent a jolt straight to my yoni. My panties were soaked, and I felt my pussy throbbing in anticipation. I licked my lips and flashed my lashes up at him. His eyes were darkened with lust, watching every movement I made.

I leaned forward and flicked my tongue against his mushroom-shaped head, causing Dre to hiss through his teeth. The taste of him alone drove me wild, and I took him deeper into my mouth, setting a pace that had him cursing under his breath.

His fingers tightened in my hair as I worked him over. I could barely get half of his length into my mouth as I took him down before it felt like I couldn't breathe at all.

*Fuck, what is he, a demigod? There has to be some reason his dick is so damn big.*

A growl of pleasure escaped his lips as I continued to go down on him, taking him deeper, harder. His eyes were shut tight, and his jaw clenched as he tried to control himself.

"Fuck, baby girl. That feels so good," he said while gasping as one hand gripped my hair while the other palmed the back of my head. His fingers gripped tighter with every bob of my head and every swirling touch of my tongue.

A moan slipped past my lips, vibrating against his spit-covered dick and sending an electric jolt through him. I felt him twitch in response inside my mouth.

I continued sucking him with fervor. His taste was addicting—masculine, sweet, and purely male—and I couldn't get enough of it.

As I sucked harder on his thick length and licked down his shaft, Dre let out a low groan of pure need.

"You're going to make me bust if you don't stop," he warned, his voice strained.

He pulled his dick out of my mouth and tugged me up by my hair. It hurt a little, but not too badly. It was the perfect amount of pain, just enough to make me want more.

Once I was back on my feet, he pulled down the straps of my red dress and smiled in satisfaction when he realized I wasn't wearing a bra.

His fingers traced the curve of my C-cup breasts. "My, my. Look at what we have here." His smile was wicked and filled with lust and promise.

Dre's hands pinched and teased my nipples, causing a sharp jolt of pleasure to shoot straight down to my center. I couldn't help but squirm against him as a low moan escaped from my lips.

"Oh God," I whimpered as he slipped one of my nipples into his mouth, rolling his tongue around it in a slow, figure-eight motion before sucking firmly.

His other hand slipped between us to the hem of my dress, pushing it up to reveal my lace thong. The feel of his calloused finger gently circling against the sensitive flesh between my legs had me moaning in anticipation.

"A thong, huh?" he quizzed with a smirk playing on his lips.

I licked my bottom lip slowly. "I wanted you to have easy access."

With a light chuckle, he pulled my thong to the side and sank into me with two fingers while rolling his thumb over my clit in a circular motion, just gentle enough to send volts of electricity through me. My legs buckled under the pleasure as if he'd siphoned command from my knees.

His mouth left my nipple and traveled upward, peppering a trail of hot, wet kisses against my skin until he reached my lips. He delivered a passionate kiss that had me seeing stars. His fingers never stopped moving, constantly driving me higher and higher until I gasped for breath against his lips.

"You're so fuckin' wet for me," he growled in my ear as his fingers picked up their pace. I could barely stand, but he was there, holding me up with his strong arms.

I moaned his name as the coil in my stomach started to tighten. "Dre…"

He pulled back slightly so he could get a better look at me. "That's it, baby girl," he murmured. "Cum for me."

His seductive voice triggered the avalanche. Pleasure crashed through me like a tidal wave, and I let out a loud cry, praying the music from the party was far louder than I was. As soon as I came down from my orgasm, Dre slipped his dripping wet fingers out of my pussy and pressed me up against the shed.

The hard exterior dug into my back and lifted me by my legs. I heard the crunch of gravel underneath his boots as he spread my thighs like smooth peanut butter on white bread. His grip tightened, fingers digging into my hot flesh as his tongue slipped between my warm folds. It was pure bliss.

I squeezed my eyes shut, relishing the moment as I wound my hips against his beard. My fingers intertwined with his locs, gently grabbing his coily roots.

"Mmm, fuck, Dre. Your tongue feels so fucking good."

My thick thighs rested on his broad shoulders, securing his head in a vise grip as I bucked forward, riding his face. I was seconds away from cumming—seconds away from every nerve ending in my body vibrating and causing a temporary disorientation so damn powerful I was sure I'd be seeing stars, planets, moons, and whatever else our solar system had to offer.

"F-fuck, Dre."

"Keep saying my name," he instructed from between my thighs.

His command turned my knees to mush. Soon after, the levee broke, and waves of my orgasm flowed through me as I looked deeply into Dre's eyes.

"I need you, Dre. I need you right now," I panted, my limbs an uncoordinated mess.

After cumming again, he stopped his lip service, looking me straight in the eyes. Those lighthearted gray orbs of his took on a mischievous, almost blissful glint. He licked his sweet lips before a smirk appeared. I watched him step forward and rest the pulsating tip on the hood of my pussy, teasing my silky folds before he pushed inside.

He slid the tip in and out of my entrance before pushing in deeper. "See, look how wet I make you. Bet no one else can make your pussy drip like this."

I shook my head. "No one but you."

Dre smirked, no doubt pleased with my answer. "Good. Because I plan to fuck you even better this time."

He pushed deeper into me. I gasped at the sudden increase in size. There was no doubt in my mind—his dick fit inside me like a hand in a silk glove, filling me up completely.

A whimper of pleasure escaped my lips. "Oh, my fucking… God…"

My head fell back against the shed, and all I could see were the stars above us and the blazing intensity in Dre's eyes. He dipped his head low and captured my nipples in his mouth, sucking and taunting me while he thrusts slowly in and out of me.

His thrusts became rhythmic, a perfectly paced dance that left me reeling for more. I clutched his shoulders, my nails digging into his skin as heat coiled in the pit of my stomach again.

"I could stay here forever," he confessed, his voice husky with his own desire as his thumb found my clit again and began to rub it in lazy circles.

"God, yes," I breathed out, barely able to finish speaking before the next heatwave rolled through me. "Don't stop, Dre. I'm—I'm so fucking close to—"

He captured my lips in a searing kiss. "Good. I want you to cream all over this dick, baby girl. I'm gonna keep fuckin' you until my balls are dripping wet."

I stifled a gasp while burying my face into his shoulder, biting gently on his skin to keep from crying out loud. I was lost in a sea of sensation. The shed, the night, the stars—everything faded into insignificance. There was only Dre, him and the delicious friction of his erection sliding in and out of me.

He tugged my earlobe with his teeth, sending shivers down my spine that lit up every nerve ending on my body. "You're so fuckin' tight," he growled against my skin, making me shudder with pleasure.

"Dre," I gasped, writhing against him, "I can't... I..."

I didn't have the words, but it didn't matter because Dre knew precisely what I needed.

His pace quickened, and his thrusts turned into forced jerks as he verged on the edge of his climax. His lips found mine again, swallowing my cries of ecstasy as another orgasm washed over me and pulled me out to sea. *How could I ever give this up?* Dre fucked me better than anyone had my entire life.

He put me down and spun me around. "Put your fuckin' hands on the wall and bend over."

I smirked, following his orders. I placed both hands above my head and arched my back so that he could reenter me from behind with ease.

"Goddamn, baby girl. Mmm," he growled against my nape while slamming into me.

All we heard were the sounds of crickets chirping and Dre's thighs smacking against my ass. He slapped my ass as my body stiffened, and his grip around my waist tightened with intensity.

"Oh fuck," he groaned, slamming into me one final time before I felt the pulsating warmth of his release filling me up.

I looked over my shoulder to see him toss his head back, throwing his long locs back in ecstasy as every muscle in his body strained.

"Fuck… fuck…" His words were lost as his breath became ragged, matching the rhythm of my own heaving chest.

"Dre." I sighed, my fingers tracing patterns on his sweat-glistened skin.

His response was a low groan, exhausted and sated. Still buried deep inside me, he collapsed onto me, pulling our bodies tightly together and curling his arms around my waist. He buried his face into the crook of my neck, inhaling deeply, as a sound of pure contentment escaped his lips. Slowly, our heartbeats began to slow, our bodies still glistening with sweat.

It wasn't just another late-night romp between us. Hell, I wouldn't even call it making love. All I knew was that Dre had devoured me, and I wanted him to keep devouring me for as long as he could.

Everything in my life seemed to change drastically in a short amount of time. I had a strong-willed woman I loved and planned to make my queen officially. I never expected Mercy to stand by me through my father's funeral or be the lifeline I didn't know I needed while my body healed completely. Her solid support and loyalty brought a sense of stability and purpose to my chaotic world of asphalt and leather.

But despite the changes in my personal life, I still had club business to attend to. As the VP of the Hell's Savages, I understood the importance of leadership and what it meant to have a strong leader at the helm. The club was about to vote on their new leader. Out of respect for my father's legacy, no one chose to run against me, but I still felt the pressure of the moment weighing on me as I stood before my brothers.

I took a deep breath as my eyes moved about the room. My

heart was in a frenzy, not just from the weight of the moment but from wondering if Mercy would be here. Her journalism work had kept her on the go ever since her article was published, and I wasn't sure if she'd be able to make it. I craved her presence more than ever. Then it happened. I spotted Mercy near the back, looking like a radiant angel.

*There she is.*

She wore a royal blue skater dress that cinched at her small waist and flared into a skirt. Her sleek, high bun and chandelier earrings perfectly framed her face. A dainty diamond heart-shaped pendant sat gracefully against her exposed, bronzed collarbone. She completed her look with strappy, nude sandals and a small clutch.

The proud smile across her face was bright enough to light up any room. Her aura was everything I never knew I needed, and it filled me with the final shot of confidence I needed. My chest inflated with a deep breath before I began my speech.

"Savages, today we stand at a crossroads. We all know my father was an outstanding president. We also know he was more than that. He was a father, a mentor, a brother, a son, a coach, a teacher, and most importantly, he was a leader. My father proudly led us with strength and taught us the value of loyalty, respect, and brotherhood. It's now up to us to honor his legacy and our code and continue down the golden path he laid for us, brick by brick, as we move forward. Let's make my father proud."

I paused, my eyes slowly observing the room, making eye contact with every member to ensure they felt exactly where I was coming from.

"I stand before you today, not as your VP, but as your brother—someone committed to the Savages and everything we stand for. I've learned a lot from my father's example, and I only wish I had the time to learn more. I know I have some big shoes to fill, but with your support, I promise to lead with the same allegiance and honor he instilled in me since day one."

The room was dead silent as the weight of my words sank in. I saw the respect and admiration in the eyes of my brothers. They began to all nod in agreement, clapping in a booming round of applause before they stood to cast their votes.

It didn't take long for the results to come in. The vote was unanimous—I was the new president of the Hell's Savages. A wave of emotions washed over me as soon as the decision was announced. It was a moment I'd both dreaded and foreseen, stepping into my father's shoes to lead the club that I loved—the club that turned me into a man. I was grateful for the trust of my brothers and a deep-rooted obligation to live up to my father's legacy. I looked up at the sky and felt a smile spread across my face.

*This one's for you, Dad. I hope I make you proud.*

Another round of applause sounded off as I stepped back up to the podium to officially accept the role.

"Thank you, everyone. Together, we'll continue to face whatever life throws our way and ensure the success and strength of the Hell's Savages remains strong."

The men presented me with my father's jacket with an updated patch to reflect my new leadership position. After putting it on, I scanned the crowd—eyes landing right on Mercy as she swiped away a quick tear, symbolizing she knew how much the moment meant to me.

After the announcement, I made my way through the sea of bikers, embracing and dapping up my brothers as I continued to Mercy. Finally, I reached her. She was waiting with a proud smile. She greeted me with open arms, wrapping them around me in a congratulatory hug. I pulled her into my arms, inhaling her light, floral fragrance before pressing my lips against hers in a long, deep kiss. The warmth of having her by my side filled the gaping hole inside my chest with a sense of completeness—something I thought would never happen in this lifetime or the next.

"Congratulations, Dre. I can't think of anyone more deserving of this than you."

I looked into her sparkling brown eyes, feeling another rush of emotion run through me.

"Thanks, beautiful. I'm glad you're here. It means a lot that you could make it."

"There's nowhere else in the world I'd rather be, Mr. President."

I paused to take a cleansing breath and gather my thoughts before I asked the question that'd been pressing on my mind. As I led the club's next chapter, I wanted her by my side.

"Well, in that case, how would you feel about being the Prez's old lady?"

Her eyes sparkled with delight. Her smile followed, along with her immediate answer.

"I'd say I like the sound of that very much."

My heart pranced with joy. With Mercy as my old lady, I felt ready to take on the challenges of leading the Savages. Together, I was sure we could face anything.

*ONE YEAR LATER.*

I couldn't believe how much my life had changed in only a year. When we met, I was a struggling journalist chasing a dangerous story, and he was the overprotective vigilante who saved my life. Now, Dre and I were off to celebrate our anniversary, the first of many. Our relationship had been a whirlwind of danger and excitement since the night we met.

We'd faced numerous obstacles together, from my high-stakes investigation into his rival MC conflicts to the tragic death of his father and taking on the role of president of the Hell's Savages. Still, the roots of our connection had only grown deeper.

Under Dre's fearless leadership, their brotherhood became more united. I continued my career in journalism, balancing the demands of chasing my next lead while playing my role as Dre's "old lady."

Despite the danger and jagged edges of the MC world, I found a sense of belonging and protection with him and his crew. Not all MCs were created equally.

The article and video footage I published about the Outlaws' sex trafficking of women gained widespread public attention, drawing the focus of the national media, the Chicago Police Department, and the Feds. The damning video evidence showed the Outlaws transporting and selling women, compromising key members of the MC and sparking immediate action from authorities to dismantle their heinous operations and pushing me into the limelight as a fearless, credible journalist.

Soon after, the Feds created a task force and raided several of their known hideouts, including their main clubhouse. During the raids, many members of the Outlaws were arrested, including their leader, Dre's half-brother.

Luckily, the task force was able to rescue several women who were being held captive in storage units, providing them with aid and rejoining the victims with their families. They also seized documents, video footage, cash, drugs, and more incriminating materials that further built the case against them.

With so much incriminating evidence stacked against them, federal prosecutors were able to charge the Outlaws with multiple counts of human sex trafficking, racketeering, and a laundry list of other offenses that led to lengthy prison sentences for all.

I snapped out of my daze when I realized we weren't headed toward our destination—an upscale restaurant known for its good food. But it was clear Dre had other plans. The sun was beginning to set as we rode his motorcycle, the cool breeze whipping my hair across my face. I held onto him tightly, feeling the familiar sense of freedom and excitement I'd gotten used to over time.

As we reached a secluded area overlooking Lake Michigan, I couldn't help but stare in awe at the view. The sky was painted with orange, pink, and indigo hues, reflecting off the calm waters below. Dre parked his bike and helped me off.

"I thought we were going to a restaurant," I said.

Dre turned to me, a playful grin on his face. "Thought this might be a better way to celebrate. Just the two of us, away from all the noise."

A warm grin spread across my face. I never imagined my life could be so magical. I'd never felt more loved or confident about my place in his world. Dre had shown me what it meant to protect and honestly care for someone. I couldn't imagine my life without him.

I leaned slightly forward to hug him with my brown orbs locked onto Dre's with a tender gaze. "It's perfect, baby. I love it."

We sat down on a blanket he'd spread out, and I sat across from Dre, dressed in a fitted graphic tee and black high-waisted skinny jeans that hugged my curves perfectly. My hair was styled in long, loose waves that fell over my shoulders, and my lips were painted with a shiny pink gloss.

Dre looked more handsome than ever, his look complementing mine with a fitted white crew neck T-shirt, black slim-fit jeans, and sneakers that made him look like an entirely different person outside of the leather jacket, dark-wash jeans, and sturdy biker boots he was always in. His long locs were neatly styled, twisted, and pulled into a high bun. On his wrist was a classic gold watch—an heirloom of his father's.

He sat with a relaxed posture, his shoulders broad and open, conveying the familiar sense of security and strength he always did. After conquering our first year together, he reached for a bottle of champagne, preparing to toast to a celebratory night.

We toasted just as the sun dipped below the view. Dre turned to me, his expression serious yet tender as his eyes softened.

"Mercy, this past year has been amazing. You've stood ten toes down by my side and showed me what true loyalty looked like in a woman. I tried to fight my feelings initially, but you've been mine since the first night I saw you. I love you more than words can say. I brought you here because I want to ask you something."

My posture straightened with a ball of nerves as my hands clasped together momentarily before placing one over my belly, trying to settle the butterflies. A smile played on Dre's lips as he reached into his pocket and pulled out a small, black velvet box. He opened it to unveil a shimmering diamond engagement ring. My breath caught in my throat as tears welled up in my eyes.

"Instead of asking you to marry me, I wanna ask you, will you take the keys to my heart? It's yours forever if you want it."

I nodded, unable to articulate words through my emotions. Dre slipped the princess-cut diamond ring on my finger, and I tossed my arms around his neck, pulling him into the warmest, tightest embrace before kissing him deeply.

"Yes, baby. A thousand times, yes."

The deep gray of his irises danced with joy, and small crinkles formed at the corners. He looked at me with such an intense gaze as if he couldn't believe his luck. His hands rested on the small of my back, holding me close.

"I love you more than words can express, Mercy."

"I love you too."

As we held each other, our future together never seemed brighter. Our love story, though quick, had proven to be true and lasting over the past 365 days. With the news of our engagement, I couldn't wait to usher in a new chapter filled with even more joy and adventure with my man by my side and the Savages at our six.

**THE END**

# A NOTE FROM K.L. HALL.

Reader,

Thank you for reading *Hellraiser: You Can Only Get This Feeling From a Thug*. If you've made it this far, I hope you'll consider telling me what you thought about the book in the form of a **five-star review and/or rating**. Don't hesitate to let me know what you'd like to see from me next. I thoroughly enjoy reading your thoughts and hearing from you as well. I'm always striving to attract new readers and retain current ones, and reviews are one of the easiest ways to attract readers. If you loved the book, tell a friend, and most importantly, let me know.

All my love,

K.L. Hall

# A WORD FROM B

Howdie!

Thank you for indulging in a BLP book. As the ambassador of Black love stories, it gives me great pleasure to provide love stories regardless of the niche. Whether you are looking for urban romance, contemporary romance, erotica, women's fiction, paranormal, fantasy, or thriller… you can find an author to read and enjoy within BLP.

Now that you've completed this book, feel free to go to our website for a list of our authors to look up on Amazon and further enjoy.

With love,

B. Love

www.blovepublications.net

# ABOUT THE AUTHOR

K.L. Hall is a national bestselling and award-winning author. As a serial storyteller, Hall has penned over three dozen titles in various genres—including African American urban fiction and romance, paranormal, children's books (as Kimberley M.), and non-fiction. Her fictional stories straddle the intersection of classic Urban and spell-binding Romance.

**Highly Acclaimed Titles:**

In the Arms of a Savage: (Peaked at #1 in Women's Fiction)

The Potomac Falls Series (Peaked at #1 and #2 in African American Erotica)

Sign up for my mailing list to stay updated with new releases, giveaways, sneak peeks, and more! Click this link: https://bit.ly/38RMpV5

**Connect with me on social media:**

Facebook: https://www.facebook.com/authorklhall

Twitter: https://twitter.com/authorklhall

Instagram: https://www.instagram.com/officialklhall/

Website: https://www.authorklhall.com

**Other novels by K.L. Hall:**

Diary of a Hood Princess 1-3

Rise of a Street King: The Justice Silva Story *(Spin-Off to the Diary of a Hood Princess series)*

Broken Condoms and Promises 1-3

In the Arms of a Savage 1-3

Built for a Savage: Blaze and Camille's Love Story *(Spin-Off to the In the Arms of a Savage Series)*

A Ruthle$$ Love Story 1-3

Fallin' for the Alpha of the Streets 1-2

The Most Savage of Them All: The Wolfe Calloway Story *(Prequel to the In the Arms of a Savage Series)*

When a Gangsta Loves a Good Girl

Caught Between My Husband and a Hustler

The Illest Taboo 1-2

To the Only Thug I'll Ever Love

A Lover's Heist: Chief and Gianna's Love Story

A Lover's Heist II: Rome and Lira's Love Story

A Lover's Heist III: Baby and Skai's Love Story

Crushed Velvet & Cashmere

Crushed Velvet & Cashmere 2

Entanglements

Never Had a Bad Boy Love Me So Good

Good Girls Always Got a Thing for the Thugs

Professor Zaddy: A Potomac Falls Novel

Bound in the Arms of a Thug: Chop & Kendyl's Love Story

Make Mine a Gangsta: The Patton Brothers Book One

Gimme a Gangsta: The Patton Brothers Book Two

A Gangsta's Love Language: A Patton Brothers Spin-Off


**Short Reads + Novellas:**

Bi-Curious: An Erotic Tale

Bi-Curious 2: Tastes Like Candy

A Savage Calloway Christmas *(Christmas novella to the In the Arms of a Savage Series)*

Lovin' the Alpha of the Streets: A Valentine's Day Novella *(Valentine's Day novella to the Fallin' for the Alpha of the Streets Series)*

Awakened: A Paranormal Romance

As Long as You Stay Down

Solace in Seven

Solace II: The Final Cut

Something Bleu

Something Borrowed

Something New

The Knight Before Christmas: A Potomac Falls Short

I'll Be Home for Christmas: A Potomac Falls Short Book II

Triggered: A Potomac Falls Novella

Wasted Off You: A Friends to Lovers Novella

Because You Don't Know My Name: A Potomac Falls Novella

Will You Say My Name: A Potomac Falls Novella Book Two

Remember My Name: A Potomac Falls Novella Book Three

Every Thug Needs a Lady: A Lady and the Tramp Retelling

Ten Things I Hate About Lovin' You: An Enemies to Lovers Novella

In Exchange: An Urban Thriller

T.A.N.: An Erotic Novella

Vegas Heaux Tales: A BLP Anthology

Hellraiser: You Can Only Get This Feeling From a Thug


**Children's Books:**

Princess for Hire

Princess Twinkle Toes & the Missing Magic Sneakers

Little One, Change the World

Adjust Your Crown: A Self-Love Coloring Book for Children of Color

**Non-Fiction:**

Authors are a Business: The Booked & Busy Course Mini Book